IFWG DARK PHASES TITLES

Peripheral Visions (Robert Hood, 2015)
The Grief Hole (Kaaron Warren, 2016)
Cthulhu Deep Down Under Vol 1 (2017)
Cthulhu Deep Down Under Vol 2 (2018)
Cthulhu: Land of the Long White Cloud (2018)

CTHULHU: LAND OF THE LONG WHITE CLOUD

EDITED BY

STEVE PROPOSCH
CHRISTOPHER SEQUEIRA
BRYCE STEVENS

INTRODUCTION BY

KAARON WARREN

A DARK PHASES TITLE

Cthulhu: Land of the Long White Clound

ISBN-13: 978-1-925759-61-7

V1.0

Printed in Palatino Linotype and Bebas Neue.

IFWG Publishing International
Melbourne

www.ifwgaustralia.com

This anthology is dedicated to Rocky Wood.

TABLE OF CONTENTS

INTRODUCTION

KAARON WARREN

If you have never witnessed IFWG Publishing's Gerry Huntman experience an epiphany, you've missed out. I was there at the 2017 New Zealand National Science Fiction Convention in Lake Taupo. I can't remember if we were talking about giant monsters, or we were talking about IFWG's anthology series *Cthulhu Deep Down Under,* or we were talking about how many good writers there were in New Zealand, but it was like a golden spotlight shone on Gerry as he said, "What about if we publish a New Zealand edition of *Cthulhu*?"

Writers flocked to him. The thing that struck me was none of them were saying, *great, a chance to be published*. All of them were saying, *here's my chance to write that story I've wanted to write for ages.*

What you hold in your hands is a testament to the excitement those writers exhibited in person, and that others displayed once word spread. These are writers who, in no particular order, love their country, love monsters, and love scaring the shit out of readers.

Jonathan Carroll in his book of essays, *The Crow's Dinner,* says, "Sometimes memories are like those huge sea creatures that for mysterious reasons rise from the bottom of the ocean and wash up on beaches." He's saying that sometimes memories emerge when they have been hidden, unnoticed, forgotten. Perhaps this is one reason Lovecraft inspires fiction so easily. The primeval basics are there, of memory and monsters, of fear of loss and madness, and of the dark heart that lies within. All we have to do as readers is tap into our own submerged stories to easily find connections with the world he created.

The stories in this book are New Cthulhu, though, with a modern understanding of how the world works and of how each of us fits into that world. The writers have adopted the realms Lovecraft created but have not taken onboard his persona, something that is very important in any re-working of the Mythos. Additionally for this anthology, each story needed to not just embody the Cthulhu Mythos, or explore an element of it, but had to be identifiably of New Zealand at the same time.

Fittingly, New Zealanders are well placed to talk of sea creatures (both the Lovecraftian type and those that are metaphor for hidden memory). Their homeland is surrounded by ocean and has huge lakes within. So perhaps it's not surprising that many of the authors have taken monsters of the deep as their jumping-off point, notably Lucy Sussex in *Ortensia and Osvaldo* and Marty Young in *Masquerades.*

Other stories explore a variety of Lovecraftian tropes, again, to modern effect. The journey into madness, a significant Lovecraft concept is used by Young, as well as by Grant Stone in *A Brighter Future,* Paul Mannering in *Memories to Ashes,* Dan Rabarts in *The Silence at the Edge of the Sea,* and David Kuraria in *Kõpura Rising.* In *The Ward of Tindalos* Debbie and Matt Cowan use growing madness plus the Hounds of Hell as inspiration. This story also explores the abyss, the depths of the ocean, as does *Memories to Ashes.* Jane Percival uses the ever-present Mythosian idea of caves, dark and unnavigable, in *The Caverns of the Unnamed One.* Percival also explores the wonderful Miskatonic University and the 'discovered book' concept in her story. Others who tap into the University are J.C. Hart in *Te Ika,* Tracie McBride in *The Shadow over Tarehu Cove* and Lee Murray in *Edward's Journal.* Murray also uses the terrifying worms of Lovecraft to drive her story.

All of the authors weave their own country's geographic attributes beautifully and seamlessly into their stories. Again, New Zealand has attributes that can reflect Lovecraftian ideas well in this regard, as this island nation is prone to earthquakes (most of the stories explore this), cracks in the earth, ancient landscapes, and age-old stories. *The Ward of Tindalos* and *Ortensia and Osvaldo* look at the violent earth, tremors and earthquakes, as do *Masquerades, The Shadow over Tarehu Cove, Te Ika, The Silence at the Edge of the Sea, Kopura Rising* and *Edward's Journal*. They all place us very clearly in New Zealand, especially *Masquerades* (the lakes) and *Memories to Ashes* (the ocean).

Culturally, the writers have reached into historical depths, too, in this book. Many of the stories talk about Māori myth, history and culture, including *Ortensia and Osvaldo, The Caverns of the Unnamed One, A Brighter Future* and *The Silence at the Edge of the Sea*.

All of these stories say to us: *Be careful in the water. Be careful in the caves. Beware the person behind you, or the one you share a home with.*

Take heed. And read.

TE IKA

J. C. HART

IZZY

I did not want to go.

The black maw of the hole did not beckon to me. If anything, it urged me to run, to throw down my caving gear and get back in the car, to speed towards town and the safety of buildings and streets and lights and noise. It was too quiet here, too still, even with the occasional bird lifting its voice in song.

"Izzy," Grace urged. "Come on. We don't want to leave it too long. We've got to be home in time for the family dinner." She hovered at the edge of the cave, helmet on and her harness in place. She looked better in the rig than I ever would, but then, she was the pro and I was just the tag-along. That summed up our whole life.

"Whose idea was this, anyway?" I asked, rolling my eyes.

"Mum wanted you to get out more. You said you'd give it a go." Grace put her hands on her hips and gave me the same glare our mother had perfected.

I think that talent skipped me entirely.

"Okay," I said, stepping towards the entrance. "You're sure it's safe?" I had to close my eyes and breathe out, long and slow. It was okay, it would all be okay. My sister was here and she would look after me. It was what sisters did.

It was what Grace did. Not so much what I did, though I wanted, so badly, not to be the screw-up everyone thought I was. I could start by following through on this. If I just tried…

"Come on, I've been here before. It's a good one to start on." She grabbed my arm and squeezed it reassuringly when I reached her side. "So, in you go!" Grace grinned, her teeth white against pink lips. Why was she wearing lipstick? Why was I thinking about that?

I took one step into the mouth of that cave. It was as if the world had been left behind until Grace stepped in and nudged me with her elbow.

"Come on, slow-poke, you know Mum hates it when we're late for dinner."

Grace moved ahead with the easy confidence of someone who'd done this time and time again, so it was a relief to be behind her, to not have her gaze on me as I found my feet and stumbled against some rocks, the spare shoes she'd given me clunky on my feet despite us being the same size.

Grace stopped and waited for me to catch up. "You ready to go?"

I let out a breath and looked where she pointed. The path wasn't too steep, winding down in a switchback fashion, littered with rocks of every size. Grace reached over and turned on my headlamp, grinning as the light splashed against her face.

"Come on. You're going to love it when we get to the bottom. There are some amazing formations."

She rambled on as we walked. Grace could speak for hours on her passions, and more than anything I think she was just pleased to be able to share this one with me, even if under duress. It wasn't that I didn't want to be there, specifically. I didn't want to be anywhere, and I didn't think any amount of beauty, or awe, would pull me from that feeling. Life was hard, my brain was my enemy, and I was too tired to fight anymore.

I almost walked straight into her back; she gave a small gasp and turned to glare at me.

I could see it there, sickly green and poisonous purple curling out of her mouth with her breath, with the word, "Watch—" She stopped. Exhaled. "Sorry, you gave me a fright, and didn't I tell you to watch out?" She gripped my arm again, harder than before. "You have to be careful, I know I said it was safe, but it's only safe if you pay attention all the time."

"Okay," I said, flinching back from the colours in the air between us. I didn't need any of that in my body; it was toxic enough as it was. "Do we have to go down?"

She nodded, then unhooked her drink bottle and took a swig. She offered it to me, but I shook my head. "We have to abseil, do you remember how I showed you?"

I nodded again, wishing I'd had that water but too frozen now to get my bottle out. We'd practiced this before, but I wasn't ready. Might not ever be ready.

"Izzy, it's going to be okay. You were great at the climbing wall, you just need to do the same here. Pretend we're back at the YMCA. You're safe. We're together. There's a permanent anchor here, and we're going to use that."

Permanent. I looked down the cliff face. It wasn't smooth, dotted with rocks of all shapes and sizes, thankfully not a straight drop.

"How do we get back up? I can't climb this." I stepped back from the edge, panic coming over me again, red and tight and twisting.

"Izzy," Grace said sharply. She gripped my chin and made me look at her. So serene. She was always so much calmer than me, as if she'd got all those genes and I'd got…something else.

"The cave has another exit so you don't have to climb up. It's going to be okay, and I promise, everything you're feeling now? It's worth it."

"Okay."

"Trust me?"

I nodded and licked my lips, so dry they felt like they would split.

"Come on." She got me hooked up and helped me to the edge. This time it was me who grabbed her hand.

"Thank you," I said, hoping that by the meagre light of our torches she could see that I meant for more than this trip. "I owe you."

She grinned as I assumed the right pose and dropped over the edge of the ledge.

"Nice form, Izzy. You've got this!" she called down to me.

The rope was strong in my hand, the fibres digging gently into my gloves, assuring me I had a good grip. I held my breath as I lowered myself, feet braced against the rocks, back leaning into the abyss. Darkness embraced me as I swung my head down so that the torch beam swept below.

"I can't see the bottom." My voice quavered.

"It's there. Trust me." Her voice was strong, steady as always. Was she ever afraid? "I've done this before, hundreds of times."

"Okay." I sent the word up like a prayer to Grace, my new goddess as I dropped into the cave. I lowered myself another few metres and looked again, but still no sign of the ground. An ache was gnawing at my chest. I was about to call up again when the rope moved in my hand. No, not the rope, the world.

Rocks clattered beside me, stumble-tripping their way to the floor.

"Grace!"

"I'm here. Just hang tight. It's a little quake." But there was a thread of fear in her voice now, it slithered down the rope and took up residence in my brain.

There was a sharp jolt and I cracked against the cliff face. My helmet protected my head, but my elbow and knees jarred against the rocks. I cried out and I knew there would be blood.

"Izzy!" Grace yelled. I looked up. Saw the light from her torch as I spun and crashed against the wall of the cliff, bright in the darkness.

"Don't fall. Help me." I didn't know if the two things could be done in tandem. Her light disappeared, but I felt a tug on the rope and I held my breath, closed my eyes. I could try to climb, but then I'd be pulling on the rope too, and that wouldn't help, would it? I didn't know. I didn't know anything. I gripped the rock face, finding crevices to dig my feet into.

The thudding of my heart was there, loud but alone. No more clatter of rocks, just my breath hitting the wall.

"I'm going to get you up," Grace's voice was comforting.

"Okay," I said.

She tugged on the rope and I shifted my foot, trying to gain some height, to help.

"Wait," she said, her voice frantic. "Don't move."

"Grace? You're freaking me out."

"I just—"

There was a rumble. The wall rippled and rolled. The sound of the rope breaking seemed loud over the roar of the earthquake and I fell and fell and fell.

I knew I wasn't dead because everything hurt. I tried to move my hand but couldn't. I realised I was stuck in mud so thick it felt like drying cement.

"Grace!" I yelled, but the only response was my voice ricocheting off the walls.

I couldn't see a thing. Were my eyes even open? Did it matter? I was stuck at the bottom of a hole with no way out. I hadn't realised until then that I actually did want to live, that despite my strange quirks and inability to hold down a job or succeed in the way normal people did, I wanted life.

A low hum filled the space. I held my breath, waiting for rocks to crash down and crush me. Tears leaked out the corners of my closed eyes, a high pitched squeal stole out of my lungs. Something tickled along my spine and I shuddered. This was fear, I told myself, fear making me feel things that couldn't be there, but then a tendril of something seemed to curl around my ankle, to tug my foot deeper into the mud. My squeal turned into a scream, which sparked like tiny glow worms expelled into the darkness.

I struggled, fighting to free myself from the mud, but my violent attempts to move only seemed to make it clamp down on me harder.

"No! No! I don't want to die in here. I don't want to die." I sobbed, sank, my chest heavy.

If I free you, will you free me?

The voice trickled into my brain with the sensation of warm honey, of melted butter, the scent of toast in my nostrils, of comfort, of home. I relaxed. I couldn't help it, it was so soothing.

Sure, I thought to the figment of my imagination. No idea how to do that, but if it gets me out of here… Wait. What are you?

It was an invitation. Something thin and sharp pierced my neck and I screamed again, light blooming behind my eyes, and then I could see…something large as it soared through the sky, its wings—no not wings, fins?—large and wide and trailing, trailing. I couldn't fathom it. It was too big, too much. Stars burst from the night sky, swimming past me so quickly, and then I could see other great beasts, wondrous, ponderous creatures moving through space, through time and infinity. They were deep blue, sparkling, shining. I didn't know. I couldn't comprehend. It was…

When Māui caught this fish I was not in the sea but in the sky and he pinned me down beneath these rocks, grew an island on me.

It unfolded in the style of the books of legends from my youth, Māui, strong and brave, half god, half mortal, his feet planted firmly on the ground, but instead of capturing the sun he was capturing this beast, tearing it from the sky with brute force. Everything collapsed back to darkness, the weight of it crushing me the same way the weight of all these rocks weighed down the beast.

"Have you been here all this time?" I asked.

So long. But I still remember.

Another flash of the stars and some ineffable, indescribable sensation that pressed my brain so hard I almost passed out. And grief. It crushed me, made me want to curl into a little ball, and then my arms were loose, my legs too, and I was folded in on myself. The images in my head of the things that were lost overwhelmed me, threatening to tip me into oblivion.

The creature pulled back, but I held my ball tight, eyes pressed shut, still seeing stars.

"Make it stop!"

Make me free.

I'd have gone crazy—Hell, I was halfway there and I'd not suffered anything like this creature had; suffering inflicted by one of my kind. That thought sped through my brain, bouncing off the pieces of me that I kept locked in boxes, stirring up anxiety.

"Anything, just make it stop. Make it stop and promise that my sister will be safe."

Everything went still, the silence so quiet that it buzzed in my ears. I dropped my hands from my head, uncurled my limbs and sat.

"I don't know how to save you," I whispered. "I don't—"

As I have been your vessel for all these years, so too shall you be mine.

Pain fired through my synapses, burning me out until everything went black.

GRACE

I paced outside the perimeter the rescue team had set up. They'd been here for hours and Izzy was somewhere down there, underneath it all. I couldn't breathe. It was my job to keep her safe and she might be dead, right now, trapped under layers of rock, her body twisted and broken the same way her mind seemed to be sometimes.

Mum was going to kill me. She'd already called, her voice so frantic I couldn't understand what she was saying. A doctor had to tranquilize her and she was at home with Dad while I paced, wearing a trench in the ground, cursing it for the terrible quake that had probably murdered my sister.

"Grace?"

I turned. It was Izzy. I inhaled, relief filling me. She was alive, she was okay, and she was crawling from the rubble in a completely different spot to where the rescue team were searching. I ducked under the perimeter tape and scrambled to her.

"You're alive," I whispered, holding her at arms-length. I didn't want to draw attention, to call for help. I needed to make sure she was okay first. She let me wipe the blood from her neck with my fingers, let me check for breaks, before I crushed her into a hug. "I can't believe it. I thought…I thought I'd lost you. I—"

"It's okay," she said. She smiled, a beatific glint in her eyes. "I'm okay. Actually, I'm better than ever."

I frowned. It wasn't the response I expected, given her predilection for anxiety. No, that was too harsh of me. It wasn't her fault that her nerves seemed to eat her alive. She was sensitive to the world around her, open and aware in a way that others didn't seem to be, and I loved that about her, even if it meant she needed my help. Even if it meant I couldn't go and live the life I'd always wanted to. She was more important.

Izzy's inability to function as a normal person had often driven Mum and Dad to distraction. I felt that if she'd had an official diagnosis of some kind it would have made it easier on all of us. I liked to think of her as a modern shaman, but then maybe that was just a coping mechanism. She was a dreamy woman, and with a little application could make some good money from her art; it just never seemed to happen.

"Over here!" I heard a shout, and then I was pulled away from Izzy as a medical team looked her over.

She had mild concussion and was free of major injury, just cuts on her limbs, her cheek, and her neck. She'd been very lucky, but the way she looked at me now…I couldn't help but wonder. Just what had happened down there to cause this shift in her manner?

It started off as just notes for the Doctor. He wanted me to keep tabs on Izzy, make sure there were no lingering effects from the concussion, to keep track of her behaviour in case she needed counselling from the trauma she'd been through.

There was some dizziness, she vomited once, and her expression was vague when I asked her about specific things. Other than that she seemed fine—more than fine, she seemed better than ever. She had gained focus, was doing some kind of research online, tinkering with some…device. I didn't know what it was and she wasn't saying a peep. She would just grin at me, with a strange gleam in her eyes, and tell me that I'd find out soon enough.

Some nights I would find her sitting on the balcony, her legs swinging over the edge and her gaze fixated on the night sky, a deep sense of yearning etching her face.

"Haven't you ever wanted to escape, to fly away?"

I bit my tongue, held back the words that would hurt her. But then she looked at me and I had to be honest. "You know I have."

"I do. That was a test." She smiled, but then she worried her bottom lip between her teeth. "I'm sorry. I know it's my fault."

"No, don't ever say that. I chose this. I chose you. You're my sister and I love you so much." I slipped my hand into hers and she squeezed it, her skin feeling drier than it normally did. "I might have wanted other things—I might still get other things—but this is what I want right now."

"I'm going to give you the universe," she whispered, eyes filled with adoration.

There was something about the way she said it that sent a shiver down my spine. As if she really meant it, in a way I couldn't comprehend.

"Come on, come inside and I'll make us some hot chocolate before bed."

"No," she said softly, letting our hands drift apart. "I want to stay out here for a bit. I'll see you in the morning." She smiled again, but I knew I was dismissed.

A week later she was out of the apartment on some furtive mission. This whole secrecy thing she had going on was driving me mad and her door was slightly ajar, so I pushed it open a little wider and peered inside.

Her room was chaos. That…machine, no, machines…took prime place on her desk and there were scattered drawings around it. I stepped inside and felt anxious as I tiptoed across to her desk. Some of the drawings were of the machines, or what I assumed were parts, maybe, for inside it. Schematics? None of it made sense to me. There were maps of the area where we'd gone caving, scrawled with distances and depths. Others were drawings of space, some familiar celestial bodies and others I couldn't identify. The artwork evoked a sense of longing, through some ineffable quality. It made my stomach ache, made me need to get out, get away from there, pretend I'd seen nothing. I turned towards the door and my mouth dropped open. I tried to take in the image on the wall. It was…

It was stars and dark skies. It was some creature I couldn't understand, sprawling across the wallpaper, trailing dust and debris behind it, leaving fire in its wake. It was dark and vibrant and vivid and more than alive. I fell to my knees, all the strength leaving me at the sight of this great beast. What was this? What was going through Izzy's mind?

I turned to see Izzy standing in the doorway. I looked at her and felt guilt and shame. I reached out my hand, my head shaking, trying to find the words to apologize for my intrusion.

"It's beautiful, isn't it?" She smiled. "You like it, don't you?" Her eyes were fixed on the wall, but all I could see was her.

Something was wrong. Something more than strange drawings and stranger machinery. She wasn't acting like Izzy, who would normally have screamed at me to get out, to respect her privacy, who could have ignored me for days in a cold fury or sobbed for a week at my invasion.

"I've never seen anything like it," I said, the only words I could think of that were honest. "Where…Where did you see this?"

She turned to face me, that glint returning to her eyes. "Under the ground. I saw a lot of things under the ground."

"Izzy, I'm worried about you." I bit my lip. "I think we should go and see someone. That you should…I don't know, get some counselling for the trauma? You were trapped underground for hours, it's only sense that—"

"Okay," she said, and then she added, "but first I want to show you something. Why don't you make an appointment for two days time, and tomorrow, I'll show you?"

Did I dare ask what? And why wasn't she fighting me? "Okay," I said, the words dull in my mouth. I didn't know how to respond to this person. I didn't know how I felt anymore.

Izzy came and gave me a hug, then ushered me from the room. "I just have to finish this little project before we can go tomorrow. I'll see you in the morning." She gently pushed me into the hallway and I heard the lock click into place.

I was drinking coffee, waiting for Izzy to emerge from her room when the front door opened. She was a mess; mud flecked her jeans from hem to knee, and dirt caked her fingers and streaked her face.

"Where the Hell have you been?" I asked, rushing to her side. "Are you okay?"

She grinned. "I'm fine. Totally fine, in fact I'm amazing. Are you ready?"

I frowned. "What, now? Don't you need to get cleaned up? Where have you been?"

"I'll show you. I promise, you just have to come. Get some sensible shoes on, and say goodbye to the real world for now."

"The real—" I shook my head. "Fine, whatever. I'll get my shoes." She was back to being dreamy, to making no sense, and in a way that was comforting. I headed down the hallway to my room to find my sneakers, pulling them on and grabbing a jacket. As I walked back to the lounge I stopped outside Izzy's room. Her desk was clear. The devices gone. I opened my mouth, but Izzy called.

"Hurry up! We need to go." That impatience was all her. I shook off the worry and followed her out the door, and downstairs to the car.

Izzy slipped into the driver's seat, taking control with an ease I'd never seen in her. She hummed an upbeat tune, and seemed not to hear my constant questions as to where we were going and why. I gave up, leaned into the headrest and closed my eyes. I'd just have to wait.

When we drew to a stop I opened my eyes and let out a gasp.

The caves. We were at the caves.

"Why? Why here?" My heart thudded and my ears buzzed. It was too soon, barely a week since the earthquake. We were still having aftershocks! Barely a week since I thought I'd lost her forever.

"Because I made a promise down there, deep in the ground, and I need to follow though. I need to show you."

Izzy got out of the car and waited for me to do the same. My knees felt wobbly, but she seemed sure and confident, and I didn't know what magic it was that had changed our roles. Was this how *she* normally felt; cautious and scared and uncertain of her place in the world?

The buzzing in my ears only intensified. I stopped walking, but she grabbed my hand and pulled me, stronger than I had ever imagined her to be. We reached the place where she'd emerged what seemed a lifetime ago, reborn into this other person that held my hand.

"Come on. We have to crawl." She let go and disappeared between two rocks, contorting her body.

"I don't want to go," I said, my voice a whisper. How could she be this brave?

"You have to." Her voice was tense, but then she sighed, relaxed her shoulders. "Remember how you made me? You knew it would be good for me, and it was. Now it's your turn to trust me. I need to give you something."

There was nothing I wanted in that hole in the ground, but I forced myself to inch forward, to twist my body, to fit myself between those rocks despite the fact it made me shudder, made bile burn at the back of my throat.

When I was through the gap the tunnel widened slightly, its walls were eerily smooth in the faint light from outside, too round and perfect to be natural. My thoughts skittered away from what that might mean.

Izzy passed me a headlamp and I pulled it on, comforted by the familiar movement. I turned the light on and the beam exposed the tunnel—it was steep, but not too steep, and Izzy was already heading down.

"You've been here before, haven't you?" I asked. My voice bounced weirdly off the walls as though the acoustics didn't quite match up to the dimensions.

"Yeah. There's just something about it."

I could hear that damned smile in her voice. I just wanted it to stop. A pang of guilt hit me; I didn't want her to be miserable, but this…joy, this inner happiness wasn't real, it wasn't her.

"How long until we get there?" The wash of emotions, the confines of the space—this place—were all crushing in on me and I needed out. But not without her.

"Soon. I promise. You're doing great."

"That's something I normally say to you." My knees hurt. My hands. My heart. I could only focus on the movement, nothing beyond my body, beyond the figure in front of me.

"I learned from the best." Izzy laughed. "Come on, just a little further."

Then there was a rush of cooler air. It wasn't fresh but it signalled open space and I pushed on, past my fear and into the open cavern. I cast my light around, trying to see why it was she'd brought me here. She took my light off me and turned on a lantern.

It was just a cave. One of her devices was propped against one of the far walls, but otherwise there was nothing here. I was disappointed. Comforted.

"Is this where you landed?" I asked.

"Almost." Izzy grabbed my hand and pulled me forward. She pointed at a shape on the ground. "There. That's the outline of me. It was mud when I landed. It's gotten harder since then."

"Is this what you needed me to see?" I frowned, not sure what purpose it served.

"Not quite."

She pulled me into a hug, held me close. I stroked her hair, inhaled the smell of her, not quite pleasant but infinitely Izzy. When she pulled away there were tears in her eyes. She pointed at the spot on the ground again. "Lie down and look up."

"Why are you crying?" I asked, rubbing my thumbs across her cheeks, wiping the tears away.

"Because I love you so much. You have no idea."

"I think I do, kiddo. Kind of love you too." I smiled at her, relaxing now. Everything was going to be okay.

I sat down in the space she'd pointed and then lay in the groove her body had left. It seemed to tighten around me, softer than I expected, warmer too. I looked up at the ceiling of the cave. Izzy switched off the lantern and I could see…

Stars. I could see the vastness of space. She'd painted it there in phosphorescence, just like the one on her wall. How had she got so high?

I tried to sit up but the ground held me tight. Something tickled the back of my neck and then pain burst through me, something else, too.

"Izzy, what did you do?" I cried.

"I wanted to give you the galaxy, Grace. You'll see things you never could have imagined. He said he would keep you safe." Izzy leaned down and kissed my forehead. "Don't struggle. It'll just make it worse." She was crying harder now as she pulled a remote from her pocket, and I couldn't move my head enough to track her movement, but she was going away, leaving me here, trapped in the ground.

"Who is he?" I yelled after her.

I am Te Ika.

I heard a beep, and then the earth rumbled, shifted, tugged at what held me. More noises, followed by another and another. Explosions. The ground shivered and shook and rocks crashed from the ceiling. I struggled, trying to cover my head, to curl into a ball, but something kept the debris from hitting me. There was a ripple, a huge shudder and then I was moving, lifting, sliding through rock, flumes of dust, walls of noise, and then clearing the ground and breaching the clouds.

The world fell away as the creature slowly absorbed me, absorbed my fears about what was happening to the island below. The hum of Izzy's tune was the only thing I could hear…

And then there were only stars.

ORTENSIA AND OSVALDO

LUCY SUSSEX

EDITOR'S NOTE: The following was found in a box of books from a deceased estate, comprising largely of runs of early twentieth-century scientific journals. They were ex-Libris Brown University, culled during the 1980s due to their lack of patronage by staff and students. Certainly the subject matter tended to the abstruse if not actually arcane. From there they fell into the hands of the Emeritus Professor of Classics, outraged at this act of "Alexandrian barbarism," as he complained to the University President. He never seems to have actually read his hoard, which he consigned to storage. Otherwise he would surely have discarded this holograph letter, extraordinary only to a particular, discerning cognoscenti. Indeed, he was notorious on campus for his opinion that literature had ended with the fall of the Roman Empire.

The letter was found inserted into the September 1913 issue of the *Journal of South Pacific Marine Zoology*. It would appear someone, perhaps the letter's recipient, had been consulting this issue, which is referred to in the text. Perhaps they were disturbed at closing time, hustled out of the library in a hurry. Overnight, the bound volume was shelved — or misshelved, since the bindings of the University serials section at that time tended to be uniform — never to be retrieved.

The letter might have been consigned to the trash can, had not several things suggested an extraordinary possibility: it had been annotated throughout, in lead pencil, by a hand which appeared disturbingly familiar, something supported by a marginal sketch, reminiscent of a much more widely known image.

It may, of course, be an elaborate bibliographic hoax, but we have made enquiries with the National Library of New Zealand, as to verifying certain details in the letter and identifying the writer. Unfortunately they are currently closed for renovation, following an earthquake. In the meantime news about the discovery has leaked out already, to the wider fan community, and interest is intense. Therefore we judge the time is ripe for its wider circulation.

To the Editor, *Weird Tales*, Chicago.

Dear Sir, Please forward the enclosed to the author concerned, as a response from a keen reader. It is under NO CIRCUMSTANCES to be published. We have quite enough trouble down here, at the other end of the world.

Yrs sincerely, Jack Smith (Capt.)

April 11 1928
c/o GPO
Wellington,
New Zealand

Dear Mr. Lovecraft,

I presume that you are a Mr., not Miss or Mrs. If I am wrong, then Madame, please forgive me. [Marginal pencil note: this is decidedly a first!] I am a bluff sea dog, who though retired, retains much of the rough and ready manners of my shipping days. Yet in the style of your writing, I think I sense the ineluctably masculine. Therefore Mister it is.

I trust that you are a man of the world, for what I have to say might seem offensive, if not actually outlandish. Plain speaking is in my nature, as is the habit of observation — of the sea and its denizens, whether from the shallows or the deeps. A man of the marine trade soon finds his life depends upon it. I am sir (you see I do not doubt it), a great reader, a habit formed during my voyages. When not on watch, or performing the various tasks of ship-worthiness (caulking, mending sails or nets), there is little to do but fish. Reading matter is beyond price in these circumstances, books being passed from hand to hand, and read until they fall apart from the usage. I have read the length and breadth of the Bible, also Darwin, Dickens and Sir Edward Bulwer-Lytton, a good companion on a dark and stormy night.

From the scientific gentlemen who took passage on my ship, I borrowed their scholarly journals, and was not ashamed to ask them to explain what was at first almost incomprehensible, but with more knowledge, became clearer. Indeed, the time that my vessel was chartered by a zoological expedition was the nigh happiest of my life, even if the ship got cluttered from stern to prow with specimens in preserving bottles. From that, I even got my name attached to a scientific paper, as co-author, thanks to certain observations I was able to contribute, about the adhesive properties of tentacles. I refer you to it, Ravenswood et al, Jnl of Sth Pacific Marine Zoology, Sept. 1913.

[Marginal pencil note: !!
Editor's note: this is the journal article within which the letter was found]

As a result of that expedition, I became a subscriber to several journals of marine studies, even a correspondent, at times. But tiring of science, religion, and the heavy volumes of the Victorians, I turned to lighter, and more modern reading. I raided my cargo: should the ship be travelling from the Americas to the Antipodes, then the lucky reader has the benefit of readable ballast. Popular magazines, even if outdated, are beyond price on that long route. Thus I discovered *Amazing*, and latterly *Weird Tales*. I have become subscribers to both, and others since. I am in short both an omnivorous and discerning reader, a tendency increasing in my widowerhood, and retirement.

Let me describe to you the circumstances in which I read your interesting story, concerning Cthulhu. I awoke one morning in my bach (for so we refer to a beachside shack), and looking out saw that the sea was calm, despite my living on one of the most violent straits known to shipping. It was a perfect day for boating, and for collecting my mail. I live in a small inlet, with only the sea, the birds, and sea creatures for company. But a man cannot live by fishing alone, and so I need provisions, of the bodily and the readerly kind. The sea is my highway, and so I took it, to the small hamlet several bays along, which boasts all that I need from civilization: a small shop, which doubles as a post office.

Returning, I hauled my dinghy past the high-tide marker, and headed for the rock pools with my prize: my reading matter for the next few weeks, which included the issue of *Weird Tales*, including your story. I stripped bare, despite a stiffish sea breeze rising, and immersing my nether regions in a deep pool, waited for my constant reader to reveal herself.

Her name is Ortensia. I have christened her such, without the aid of holy water but her own domicile of the briny. The name came from a lady, though some might not call her such, encountered in my youth. Nay, not a mermaid, but a friend to seamen, residing in a well-frequented port. What she gave me was hardly the love of a good woman, but an experience beyond pearls. What a grip sir, she had on her! And as you are a man of the world I think you will know to what I refer.

[Marginal pencil note: I am not sure that I do]

I never replicated it since, though I wished for it sorely with my late, poor wife, a most un-apt pupil in that area. Now, I waited, until upon my foot I felt a delicate touch, a nuzzle, as if from a parrot, but sub-marine. It is my opinion, though not backed up by science yet, that though she may recognise me by sight, to be absolutely sure she tastes my skin. Now her own pelt responded, changing subtly from the grey of the shell-grit and rocks, to something approximating the shade of my pale and leathery hide. I put out my hand, she put out 1/8th of her equivalents, and we squeezed each-others' flesh, as if meeting in the street. What a grip she has—and not only of my hand. That is why I call her Ortensia.

[Marginal pencil note: I think I am beyond exclamations at this point. And almost beyond reading any further…though the missive strangely compels me]

I was at one time inspired to compose a letter on the subject of my two Ortensias, which I sent to Mr. Havelock Ellis. I thought he would find it of interest, given his specialised scientific interests, and his sojourn in Australia. However, he never replied. I cannot imagine why.

Ortensia the second may or may not recognise her name—for there is much I do not know about her, she being a smallish female of the octopoid ilk, in scientific parlance *Pinnoctopus Cordiformis*. The Māori, the original inhabitants of these isles, call them *Wheke*. But she lifts her domed head above the waters, and peruses me, with those eyes, so alien, with their horizontal pupils, like the goats, and yet so disturbingly human in their gaze. I do not know what she wants from me, beyond our brief tussles in the water. But I do know that when I open a book and start reading, aloud as is the habit I developed on ship, when amusing the illiterates among my crewmates, for all the world she seems to be listening. And if I should stop untimely, in the middle of a page, well, then she will reach out and nudge me, to continue.

Thus I opened this latest issue of *Weird Tales*, and flicked through it, seeking something to amuse my constant audience. My gaze stopped short at the mention of the sea, and then further on, at the mention of New Zealand. Though we be Pacific neighbours, even if distant, it is rare that my trio of islands gets mentioned over the seas, except when the volcanoes misbehave. And so I read, and read on, to my audience of birds, mussels and Ortensia.

Have you ever visited our distant lands? I would hazard not, nor to Australia either. I am sure you would not have seen a copy of the *Sydney Bulletin*, which you mention—we refer to it as just the Bulletin. It is not a daily newspaper, with items of current calamity, as you suggest, but more a weekly journal of opinion, generally strong, relating to literature, politics, mining speculation and the like.

It is certainly true that ships dock at Darling Harbour, and you state the location of the Museum in Sydney correctly. That I would say you gleaned from access to a well-stocked library. You give an appropriate location, both latitude and longitude, for your sunken city, not like Sir Arthur Conan Doyle, who once situated a New Zealand farm out in the Tasman Sea. I wrote to him about that, too, and he responded, quite courteously.

But there is much in your story that imagination cannot supply in the absence of experience. I would think your narrator a man of very poor observation if he could voyage from San Francisco to New Zealand without noting the changes in the Pacific, the weeds, the depths, the different birds. And then has he nothing to say about the mighty Atlantic, on his trip to Oslo? It beggars belief to me that a man would sail into three magnificent harbours, that of Sydney, Auckland and Dunedin, and have nothing to say about them. Well?

I also add, knowing Dunedin, that the place is too far south to be the base for an island trader. Auckland would suit the purpose far better. And it is cold for most of the year, chilled by Antarctic blasts, such as are generally eschewed by Kanakas, who being Melanesian, prefer the tropical climes. Unless perhaps by Kanakas you meant the Māori, a misconception to which they would take exception, and violently too. Such people of colour as are in Dunedin – the place tending to the Scottish – are generally only temporary, as with the black and white minstrels, popular there. You also mention the woods, but the parlance here is bush.

And being a man of scientific pedantry, I wondered if your god Cthulhu was physiologically possible, given that tentacles and wings, even scaly, are very unlikely to exist on the same creature. Does your deity owe more to Heraldry than to nature?

[Marginal pencil sketch, similar to the well-known image, but without wings. It is then crossed out]

But then as you write, these nightmare beings seep down from the stars, where the rules of life are likely to be not as we ken it, not at all. I could show you nightmares from another direction altogether, which would chill your blood…

But I get ahead of my narrative, and that is something no storyteller should do.

In short, though I have some niggles, otherwise I found "The Call" engrossing, providing much for further reflection. I read it, as it is a long tale, over the course of several days, in my rock pool, with Ortensia. As she did not turn bright red, the usual habit of her species when annoyed, it clearly did not displease her. Indeed, when I finished, she would not pause for an embrace, but immediately hide herself in a hole in the rock, where she would settle, turning herself the matching shadow-grey, deep in what I fancy passes with her for thought.

But now my tale must turn to darker matters. Specifically, Osvaldo. He is not a creature of the shoreline rocks, his usual hunting grounds being several bays away. I named him, as I did Ortensia, for the O. The original Osvaldo was human, a shipmate of mine many years ago, a strapping youth from the South Americas. That they may have had a grip in common I know not, for though seamen have the habits of improvisation, any port in a storm, the original Osvaldo was a very hot-tempered young buck, best avoided – though easy on the eye.

Are Osvaldo and Ortensia acquainted? I suspect so, from the knowledge that so much in the sea is interconnected. But I hope they keep their distance, not only from jealousy, but also from the likelihood that he would either eat or mate with her. Or both. He is a large example of his species, she, petite. And did you know that after Octopi mate, they die – not only the male, as with the arachnids, but both of them, for having mixed their intimate matter in their pearlaceous eggs, they are surplus to nature's requirements? What would become of human civilization, should we do the same?

I sought a fish dinner…and not wishing to deprive Ortensia of some prey, I rowed to the next bay along, and cast my line. Not expecting a bite immediately, I took *Weird Tales* with me, intending to peruse the other stories in the issue. I had my boat, my bait, and my reading, and on a day of bright sun and calm sea, what more could a man ask for, except a tasty catch?

In a little while I felt a tug on the line, hauled at it, and it hauled back – too strong for a mere fish. Then I saw the water below my line boil red, a large writhing mass of tentacles. Osvaldo had grabbed my catch! I threw the contents of the bait pail at him, but in his red rage he thought it poor pickings. I bent over the side of the boat, and pulled hard on the line, as if in tug of war. Osvaldo responded with a jet of sea-water from his siphon, aimed precisely and nastily at my eyes. In a rage now myself, I threw the first thing that came to hand – the precious copy of Weird Tales. It hit the water – and in an instant Osvaldo had released the fish and was shovelling the precious pages into his maw.

[Marginal note: A nightmare to chill my blood indeed]

Well I took my fish home, a little gnawed though it was, and ate it in poor spirits. I tried reading the other magazines in my mail, but they had little interest. I wandered along to my rock pool, but Ortensia was either absent, or so well camouflaged that even I, her habitual companion, could not sight her. And ended that day, with me most out of sorts.

The next day produced lead-grey skies, and a dead, sullen calm. I wandered across the sand, beachcombing as usual. Finding few pickings, I took the boat out, avoiding Osvaldo's lair, for I was still angered at him. My destination was a beach of our black, volcanic pebbles, frequented by a seal colony. Once I would have hit the beasts on the head, for the sake of their fat, and their silky pelts, but now I let live. When a man is sick at heart, as I was, the sight of their chubby pups at play in the surf can cheer immensely.

As I rowed, I began to feel a sense of creeping unease. The sea lapped greasily at my gunwale, the water messy with weed, or even mud. Was it possible I had slept through a minor earthquake, as is common in these shaky isles? Things were either too quiet, or too busy. I would appear to be utterly alone, but then flocks of gulls would wheel high in the sky, shrieking, or shoals of fish dart underneath the boat, in agitation, or so it seemed. I turned around once, fancying myself watched, but all I could see was the far distant Kaikoura Mountains, looming across the strait, their topmost reaches pale with snow.

So high! And then, offshore, a precipice, heading into the watery deeps. Of us warm-blooded creatures only the whales take that long road downwards, and what they see they do not tell us. Dark cities, such as in your story, and even darker denizens? I have witnessed a whale washed dead on the beach, with on its hide the marks of suckers, as with Ortensia and Osvaldo, but far bigger, scars left by a colossus, a Kraken as the old-time sailors called it.

I reached the seals, but found no play, with the entire colony, battle-scarred bulls, sleek females and their young, on the beach, as if they were boats drawn up high out of the reach of a stormy sea. They were clumped protectively, staring anxiously at the waves. To get between a seal and the sea, their retreat, is folly, I knew that. But from the way these creatures acted, it was as if the sea itself had become a threat.

Confused and disconsolate, I rowed back. But then suddenly my boat was bumped from beneath, nearly causing me to lose an oar. It slapped back onto the sea and I beheld the black and white face of a Killer Whale, the sea-wolf, with behind it the fins of several of its fellows. I waved my oar threateningly, lest it try and upset me again. Their faces appear painted, like those of blackface performers, without expression beneath. But I would swear this beast looked frightened — of what, when his species are the top predators of the sea? Then he slapped his tail, soaking me, and he and his pod shot off, for all the world as if they were pursued.

I had intended anyway to give Osvaldo's inlet a wide berth, but at its mouth, I stopped, at first curious, then becoming aghast. In my travels I have witnessed the boiling mud pools in the volcanic regions, and the surface of the bay was equally as active—and blood-red. I had seen water that colour before, but stagnant and putrid, invaded by algae. Or, on my one visit to Iceland, when I witnessed a pod of small, harmless whales driven into a cove and slaughtered, weltering in a mix of seawater and their own blood. Truly we abuse the sea, and its creatures, until I fear one day they will have a dire reckoning with us. As I realised at what I was looking, I felt that time had come. The sea was the colour of not one angry octopus, but hundreds, writhing and seething, an army being rallied for invasion, or so it seemed. Quickly I took my leave, praying not to be followed.

At my bay it was calm again, thank goodness. I leapt from my dinghy into the shallows, and ran to my rock pool, still brandishing an oar, as if I needed a weapon. "Ortensia! Ortensia!" I shouted. I jumped bodily and rudely in, and when I could not see her immediately, started poking at the rocks with the oar's end. "Ortensia!" It met pulpy resistance, and then she changed her hue, charging at me, in an instant changing from rock-grey to red, her siphon drenching me with not only water, but the black of her ink.

I ran, near blinded, back onto the land, and did not stop, stumbling and panting over the hills of the coastal scrub, and inland. At one point I encountered some moonshine makers, with a still, and bought some of their hooch. Finally I passed out in a ditch, and awoke the next morning at dawn, head splitting but alive.

I have not dared go back to my bach since. What may be happening out in the strait I do not know. I fear I may have to become a landlubber, which at one time I would have regarded as a fate worse than death.

It is only fair, Mr. Lovecraft, that I let you know what has happened. I have gradually realised, over the years, that the Octopi have more intelligence than they are generally credited with, and that they communicate in subtle but efficient ways. Ortensia was, I fear, too apt a reading pupil; and Osvaldo, whom now I suspect was her crony all the while, devoured your work both as food, and as us humans do, for information. Like the cult devotees in your story, these Cephalopods hear the call of Cthulhu. It is up to you, Mr. Lovecraft, to silence that call forthwith, or as you said in your story (see, I can remember it almost verbatim): Loathsomeness will rise from the deep and decay spread over the tottering cities of men.

I remain,
Yours very truly
Jack Smith (Capt.)

[Marginal note in pencil: If this is Klarkash-ton's work, very droll, and I must in revenge hoax him forthwith. If not, then I really should communicate with Captain Smith, even if I do put audacity before caution.]

THE SILENCE AT THE EDGE OF THE SEA

DAN RABARTS

"First place in the world to see the sun rise," the pilot says into the radio, as the tiny islands and their scatterings of sea-swept rocks emerge from the murky ocean.

Augustus Shandon nods, but doesn't reply. He's not sure which has irked him more, the interminable flight, this flyboy's incessant chatter, or the thought that here, at the edge of the world where the sun first rises, so too does the sun first set. The day is getting on, foreshortened for Augustus Shandon by the curvature of the earth—lost time he will never recover—and soon it will be night.

The Sunderland descends, Chatham Island swelling but never quite filling the windscreen. From the air, the island resembles the profile of some beastly skull, Petre Bay a toothy maw hanging open, Te Whanga Lagoon the great empty eye-sockets of a leviathan laid out to rot on the ocean floor, this remnant of its being the only fragment to graze the mortal world. As they make their approach, the blustery grey South Pacific dominates the horizon. The sea is reflected in the glowering sky, dwindling these scraps of rock and sand and tree to insignificance on the ocean's vast canvas.

The flying boat shudders with the impact of touchdown, the pontoons beneath the wings throwing up rooster tails of spray as it settles in the lagoon. Acres of brackish water ringed by swampy reeds and rugged, desolate hill country surround the Sunderland. The massive propellers roar and whine as the pilot guides the flying boat towards the floating dock. By the time the plane is moored and Augustus and his bags have been offloaded, he's still thanking his lucky stars they didn't run aground. Who knows what may lurk beneath these waters, waiting for a chance to slice open the belly of such a lumbering goose? So ungainly a thing, so cumbersome up close, yet out over the endless waters of the Pacific it felt tiny. Despite the evidence of decades, Augustus still finds it unnatural that a thing so unwieldy as an aeroplane can achieve and sustain flight. Surely the laws of physics should defy this aberration, if only because of the insult to the grace and beauty of those creatures with wings, which make the sky their home. What right have we to claim their domain for our own, there to joyride and make our wars and fancies? Must we, with our human arrogance, challenge the very heavens?

The driver from town throws his bags onto the back of a small, smoky truck. He's Māori, yet he has the red-tinged hair that suggests traces of Moriori in his blood, those people who claim to be the rightful inhabitants of this place they called Rēkohu, Misty Sun, before they were all but wiped out by another grand human invention: genocide. Augustus climbs into the cab.

"Welcome to the Chathams," the driver says as he gets behind the wheel. "First time, eh?"

"Hmmmph," Augustus says, hoping to derail this pointless chatter that other people so insist upon, filling all the nooks and crannies of day and night with a constant drivel of meaningless inanity. Why could people not just appreciate the silences for what they are? Why always with the talking?

"I'm Will," says the driver over the motor's growl as he throws the truck into gear, and it bounces off down the rutted trail alongside the lagoon. "We don't get a lot of visitors out our way. Not really a holiday destination, though if you ask me there's no better place in the world. You like mutton-bird? You're gonna love the mutton-bird. What you here for anyway?"

Augustus grits his teeth. His mother taught him to be polite. "I'm here to do research. Anthropological. I shouldn't be long."

"Scientist, eh? Yeah, we get a few through. Taking an interest in our little scrap of nothing out here. You studying the whales? They migrate up through here. My cousin Hemi's got a boat, he can take you out if you need a charter."

"I'm sure," Augustus mutters. Clearly, this far from civilisation people don't even know the meaning of the word anthropology. "No, not whales. Nothing nearly so extravagant. I have arranged use of a vehicle for my work."

"No worries, bro. That'll be me."

"No, not a driver, a vehicle. My work is highly confidential. I must go about it alone."

Will laughs, a throaty sound like a pig choking. "Not a lot of spare cars out here, eh. Don't stress, I'll sort you out, getcha where you need to be. My lips are sealed, eh."

Augustus glowers.

The truck rises and falls along the narrow road between the low hills and the swell of the ocean. Is there nowhere on this godforsaken island where the watery horizon does not dominate the view? Is there nowhere one might hide?

The truck pulls up outside the tavern in Waitangi, the Chathams' largest town and still barely more than spit in the wind on a winter's day. Augustus has never been more pleased to reach a bar, until he gets inside. The stink of stale beer and old cigarette smoke is enough to put him off wanting to eat for a week. Will lugs his suitcases to the upstairs guest room while Augustus signs in with the elder gentleman at the bar, who looks as dilapidated as the building.

"Kitchen opens at five," the publican tells him, "closes at seven. Menu's on the blackboard." He fixes Augustus with rheumy eyes through a mask of weathered, leathery skin, dark and scarred like a man who has lived most his years under the salt-harsh sun of the rolling sea.

Augustus nods and glances at the blackboard: fish, fish, more fish, mutton-bird and steak, all generously served with potatoes and vegetables, as if potatoes were not already a vegetable.

"Just give Arty a yell when you need a lift, bro," Will says, waving as he heads out the front door. "I'm never far away. Can't really be far away out here, eh?" He laughs again, that twisted sound.

Augustus shudders, and climbs the staircase to his room, which, of course, overlooks the sea. He yanks the curtains closed and sinks onto the hard bed, relishing the confines of the four walls, yet through the window rumble the waves as they roll against the waterline just outside. It's there, always there.

Taking a deep breath, Augustus busies himself with checking his things, arranging his books and equipment. He fills his leather knapsack with a journal, sketchbook, reference notebooks, pens and pencils, maps of the island, charts of the surrounding ocean. Trenches and canyons plunge into unknown depths just a few miles from the shallows of the Chatham Rise, eternally cold and unknown, deeper than comprehension. Yet something drew the Moriori here, so long ago. Something kept them here, right up until their final days.

It is late afternoon when Augustus leaves his room and dares to walk the streets of Waitangi, treading the wharf, the wind brisk in his face. This place ought to be desolate, forgotten, abandoned. Yet it persists. The hulking freighters trimmed in rusty streaks return to dock for the evening, offloading crates of fish layered in ice and salt. The sea sustains these people, just as it did when the Moriori chose this inhospitable archipelago in the middle of the unrelenting ocean as their home. Some say they arrived here fleeing the Māori, some say the Māori followed them here, one people hunted nearly to extinction by another. Whatever the truth of it is, the Moriori are gone now, glimpsed only in bloodlines, a curve of the nose, a shade of hair. Yet Augustus is not interested in their end, however brutal or bloody. He is interested only in what drew them here to begin with.

Augustus returns to the bar and orders the steak and a cold beer as night finally settles in. Will appears and pulls up a bar stool beside him. "Take you out in the morning, eh. Where you headed?"

Augustus lets the beer cool his throat before replying. "Hapupu."

Will is very still for a long moment. "Can't take you there, bro."

"I merely wish to study your dendroglyphs, the carvings left in the trees by your ancestors. If you can't take me there yourself then take me to the property owners and I will ask permission of them instead."

"Can't. It's tapu. Only family can go there. I hope that's not all you came to do, mister, because if it is you wasted a trip."

Augustus sips more beer. He'd rather not but in a place like this it helps him fit in with the locals, at least a little. "Then perhaps I might start at Point Munning."

"Shit, bro, you trying to fall off the map or what?"

Point Munning lies at the extreme north-eastern tip of Chatham Island, a low, flat, desolate scrap of windswept rock and sand populated by hardy grasses and a few determined trees bent permanently to the shape of the constant sea breeze. Beyond it are thousands of miles of the Pacific Ocean. Standing on this point, Augustus is surrounded on three sides by the pulsing rise and fall of the sea, as if somewhere beyond the horizon in those sudden vast depths something breathes, its sleeping motions stirring the water to fright. He imagines himself an intrepid explorer, some several hundred years earlier, having successfully crossed the harrowing stretches of the South Pacific in a fragile waka built of wood and flax, thinking he had found a new world to call their own, only to have those hopes dashed by crossing the island and finding here, barely a day's walk from where they made landfall, that the world once again ended in an infinity of waves. This land was no new Aotearoa, no land of the long white cloud and promise of bounty, but one of misty sun and eternal sea.

Augustus draws his journal from his knapsack and starts to sketch and take notes, while Will sits in the truck atop the hill where the track ends. His driver is keeping out of the wind, eager to be gone again. Augustus hopes his presence will be required elsewhere, and soon enough, his wishes are granted. The radio in the cab crackles, and Will replies. After a brief conversation, Will opens his door. "Hey, I gotta go do a couple things. You right for a bit?"

Augustus waves dismissively, and continues to scrawl until the sound of tyres on gravel dies away. Then he packs his things and sets off south along the coast. Nothing is far away, at least, and this is why he got such an early start this morning. Will may think they're too far from Hapupu to walk, but Augustus Shandon marched across northern Africa in service to Queen and country. This little tramp is but a breath of air, a stretching of the legs.

In this flat part of the islands, the tumbled farmland soon gives way to the wide, graceful curve of Hanson Bay, and the landscape sinks into a valley of low bush and tall, slim trees. The walk has taken him three hours, and no doubt by now his absence will have been noted. Maybe the locals will presume him drowned and give him up for dead before they suspect him of defying their wishes and entering the sacred grove without permission, but he doubts it. Time is short.

He stands alone on the sands of the bay, the ocean before him and two lakes at his back, and he imagines how it must have felt to be the first man standing here, seeing what he sees, hearing what he hears: the long, drawn hush of the ocean breathing. The insignificance of blood and skin and hair in the face of that great emptiness, stretched out before the constant wind.

"I am here," he shouts, challenging the massive breathing silence. "You called, and I came."

The sea doesn't answer back, not in words. Only in its touch, wrapping the wide crescent of sand like a lover running her finger up the curve of his throat. He shudders, and turns to the bush behind him. Just as someone long before him turned from that hush, that touch, and knew he must capture what he saw, what he felt. Augustus walks up the sand into the shadow of the sacred trees they call Hapupu.

Augustus walked up the sand into the shadows of the sacred halls they called Tut-Hasputet. Stepping from beneath the anvil of Egypt's punishing sun was a relief, even though his heart pounded in his mouth with the knowledge that, officially, this place was off-limits to enlisted men. But since this war had dragged him so far from home, and his only reward had been to bear witness to a lifetime's worth of suffering and death, why would he not take this opportunity to see something curious, something that mattered, a glimpse of a past more ancient than anything he might ever see back home in quaint, rural New Zealand.

It had cost him all his cigarettes to buy his way past the guards stationed before the ruins, but luckily the army kept the boys in nicotine sticks and he didn't smoke, so it was a price easily paid. From his knapsack he pulled his clunky standard-issue torch and descended the tunnel in its wan light, clambering over fallen rocks and the smoke-charred debris left in the wake of the shelling. The silence beneath the earth, broken only by his footsteps and shallow breathing, stretched out dark and deep, drawing him down.

The silence beneath the trees, broken only by his scuffing footsteps and laboured breathing, stretches out dark and deep, drawing him in. The kōpī trees arch and loom, swaying in the sea breeze, and the symbols glare at him from where they were carved into the bark, long ago. The glyphs may be birds, some scholars say, since birds were such an important factor in the Moriori's survival. Others suggest the glyphs are the faces of ancestors, or heroes. But Augustus Shandon had seen something completely different when first he had read the works published by D.R. Simmons on the meanings of the rakau momori, and seen the accompanying sketches and photographs. Contorted, maybe, by time and the nature of trees to grow and change and heal, but there in the pages of the *Journal of Ethnographic Sciences* he had seen the same faces he had first chanced upon in the dust-dark tunnels of Tut-Hasputet, outside Cairo.

He had come home from the war with only one thing on his mind: to return one day to Egypt, to see those places again, to touch once more the faces of the gods he had found. Yet despite securing his university education, work opportunities for anyone passionate about archaeology or ethnography were few and far between in post-war New Zealand, unless you were already part of the social elite. Augustus was not so privileged, merely a working class lad conscripted to service who had survived the war mostly unscathed, in body at least. Instead he had worked menial research and administrative jobs at Auckland's tin-pot university and libraries, reading of others' far-off discoveries in the periodicals and hating them all for their successes; until Simmons' discovery, on an island just a few hours distant from his home, had led him here.

Augustus draws a fountain pen from his pocket as he moves from one kōpī to the next, craning his neck to view the shapes carved in the bark. It is so much more beautiful than he could have anticipated. Not ancient, like the drawings in Tut-Hasputet, but undeniably of the same dream-state origins. These are living trees, and so they will grow and mend and wither and die, like people, and Augustus cannot help but grieve for all the rakau momori already lost, fallen to wind and rot and age. He is surrounded by the kōpī and their vulgar yellow fruits when he sees it. The one he came here to find, that which had called to him. He leans against another tree and sucks in breath at the sight of the carving, a cold sweat on his brow as the image takes him back fifteen years, to those forbidden graves in the Egyptian desert. With shaking hands, he opens his palm and starts to draw.

With shaking hands, he opened his palm and started to draw. In the torch's dim light, Augustus could just see his sweating palm, and the shape peering back at him from the crypt wall. The fountain pen moved in shaky lines, copying that face, a smile as wide as an ocean, the thread of ribs and long curving limbs, eyes like hollow pits. Would that the army had given them all journals so he might have sketched this discovery. Ink, they had aplenty, but paper was hard to come by. So he drew the face, the suggestion of a body, on the soft flesh of his hand, cursing as sweat marred the ink, distorting the clarity of the miracle before him. This image on the wall was a crude rendition, the attempts of a benighted barbarian to capture this essence in the trappings of art to represent something so much greater, yet constricted by the hard edges of stone and chisel. There was more to this carving, buried in the inadequacies of human comprehension and expression, so limited at the best of times.

At once, Augustus understood his error. Like the artist who had stood here long before him, straining and sweating, Augustus was trying to capture what he saw with human tools, inert, fallible brushes on a fixed pallet, when he sought to capture something that pulsed and breathed. As he slipped his pen away and drew his knife, he heard a deep rumble, like an artillery shell falling somewhere far away, or a sigh rising up from within the very earth itself.

As he slips his pen away and draws his knife, he hears a deep rumble, like an echo of distant artillery, or a sigh rolling up between the trees, from their very roots. The scars stand proud on his palm and wrist, highlighted by ink, the face grinning up at him just at it did so long ago. It writhes and stretches as he flexes his fingers. He touches the tip of the knife to the ink, and begins to cut.

He touched the tip of the knife to the ink, and began to cut. Shallow at first, a thin tracery of blood suggesting the shape, a silhouette within an outline. There was no pain, just a rushing in his ears.

There is no pain, just a rushing in his ears, like all the winds of all the seas are rushing past him, dashing into oblivion against the vast nothing of the ocean. The trees bend and shake, their graven images snapping back and forth as if they seek at last to take wing from these mortal prisons.

Blood runs in thick rivulets down Augustus' fingers, the knife trembling as he opens up the old scars, remembering how they found him there, dragged him out, ignoring his pleas that he wasn't yet finished, he still had to do the eyes. He remembers how they took his knife and his gun and wrapped him up to heal. When he tried to rip the bandages off, tried to take a scalpel from a passing tray in the hospital and finish the necessary cuts, they put him in a special jacket and shipped him home. Those people had no idea what they had ruined, what they had taken from him. By the time he was cleared to leave the hospital, he could no longer visualise the face, the eyes. The memory was blurred.

Until now. This time, there is no one to stop him.

The eyes do not form a part of the tableau of puckered scar tissue covering his hand and wrist, but it's clear what he thought were ribs may in truth be tentacles, that these long narrow eyes through which he can see a deep sinking eternity may indeed be those of wheke, the octopus, who would also have been an essential part of Moriori life in these parts, just as they were to the ancient peoples of the Mediterranean.

He sets the knife to the unmarked skin near the centre of his palm and cuts one short, sharp gash where an eye should be. Such a neat little slice, yet it says so much. Looking into the trickle of blood that leaks from the cleanly separated skin, Augustus can see the tears of the universe, and the depths within.

"Mister Shandon."

Augustus whips his head up. No, not again. Through the trees, men with rifles. Just like they came the first time—traitorous curs—when they found him before he had completed the drawing, the cutting. He takes a step back. There's Will, and two others he can see, perhaps more through the trees. The eyes of the dendroglyph look back at him, and he can see their completeness, their immensity. He stands on the verge of something huge, the greatest of human discoveries. The edge of a pit within which swirl the leviathan colours of the infinite. He will not have it taken from him again. He sets the knife to his palm, to the last open patch, where the final eye belongs.

"Told you you're not to come here, Mister Shandon," Will says, advancing, the rifle held low but oh so very there. "This place is tapu. People come here, bad things happen. Drop your knife."

Augustus regards the approaching men. Sees how their eyes are downcast, looking only at the ground, at the bases of the trees, not up at the marvels that surround them.

"How can you deny what you have here?" he sputters, the knife still poised upon his skin, ready to make the final incision. "These are not simply childish etchings, they are more than mere art. They speak to a higher existence, to that which called out across the trackless ocean to your forebears. Showed them this place. Don't you see?"

"Put the knife down, Mister Shandon."

He stares at them, aghast. How can they be so blind? Can't they hear the siren song? Can they not taste on the wind how the ocean calls?

He makes the cut. The pain is distant, but final. The knife drops into the leaf mould, blood spattering where it falls, a pattern like the spiral of nebulae against the black. He looks at his palm. The eyes stare up at him, deep and dark and hollow and weeping with the joy of blood, and they blink their approval. The ocean roars.

Augustus holds up his bloodied hand so they can witness the truth for themselves. "See!" he cries, eyes shining with triumphant glee. "This is what was needed!" He backs away from the men with the guns, towards the tussocks and grasses and the border between land and sea.

Will brings the rifle up to his shoulder, sighting down the barrel. "Stop walking, Mister Shandon. You've done a very foolish thing."

But fear is a foreign concept now. How can he be afraid when the immensity of all creation surges beneath his feet? He is but a mote of dust, yet he shines bright in the light of a star he cannot see. Not yet. That star, that light, resides beneath the waves, has lain here sleeping for so very long; and in its sleeping, it has dreamed, and its dreams have crawled up through the waves and made their homes in the nightmares of men, who have marked the trees with their terror, their warnings.

Only because they do not understand, he thinks.

Augustus Shandon does not fear. He has given the dream life, his own life. He drips it in a steady, coagulating ooze onto the grasses at his feet, trails it in the sand, like breadcrumbs leading from a dark forest back to a safe place. He tops the dune.

The ocean was always a constant breathing thunder in his ears, but now it has changed. Now it is a hiss, like the sound behind silence on the radio waves. Will and his companions hesitate, their mouths open. Augustus turns.

The tide has drawn back. The seafloor lies glistening, exposed like flesh beneath skin peeled back by the scalpel, and along the line of the bay, the ocean stands in a rising wall. It arches over the island, an open eyelid, and in the swirling murk of the sea as it stands and gathers and grows shimmer the lights of ancient stars.

Augustus stumbles through the sandy grasses towards the sea, a door opening to greet him. The men with their rifles forgotten let him go. The silence is now so huge it swallows Augustus, soaking up all thought. His boots sink in the wet slurry of sand, thick with seaweed and gasping fish.

Of course, when you are so ancient and wise and you flee across the void to find a place to hide, where better than deep beneath the waves? And when you can perceive that in the fullness of time, these fledgling mammals who hoot and shriek and hit each other with rocks will grow to dominate the lands, to wither each other with their wars and avarice, eventually to burn up in the heat of their own flame, would you not bide your time until the dawn of their collapse nears, even if those days may be drawn out by a measure of eons? What matter, if you can sleep? But in sleeping, yet you dream, and still you desire the adoration of the lowly, still you desire the satiation of warm sacrifice: perhaps an animal, or a person, or an entire race. And so your needs infect those with a mind clear enough to hear you above the noise of the world, to hear the silence that hisses between the stars, that silence you found in the deep places between the continents, wrapped in its skin of sea. A place into which those sacrifices might be cast to soothe your sleeping hunger, and never be seen again.

"I heard you, and I have come," Augustus cries, halfway across the bay now, the wall of water towering ever higher. "What do you desire of me?"

He raises his hands in supplication. This will be his moment.

For this, he has lived. In the wake of all the madness humanity has wrought, he will usher in something new, something beautiful, to sweep away the desperation and ennui into which the world has fallen.

He doesn't hear the gunshot, only feels the shattering of bones, the spray of blood hot on his cheek as a bullet passes through his upraised hand, destroying the glyph he has so carefully nurtured, carved, and brought to life in the pulsing of his own heartbeat. He wants to scream, but there is nothing in his throat but the great silence that has drawn him in.

Yet the circle has been closed.

The thing that lurks, slumbering, the thing that has opened one bleary eye and tasted the salt of sacrifice, knows that it is loved.

The eyelid raised over Augustus Shandon blinks, the presence behind it barely twitching in its millennia-long sleep, and the ocean collapses back into the bay. Augustus hears no more but the roar of the winds that howl through the empty spaces between the stars as the waters fall down upon him, and draw him hungrily into that deep, eternal throat.

THE CAVERNS OF THE UNNAMED ONE

JANE PERCIVAL

Prologue

I'm floating up through the clouds, as if I'm a plume of thistledown. Caressed by pleasant warmth. I barely recognise that sweet feeling, so long has it been. My eyes are tightly closed and yet beyond the lids there is bright light. Dazzling. I try to raise an arm to shield them, but the limb is weak and falls back against my chest.

Where am I? Vomit pushes its way up my throat. I can feel it dribble between my lips and… Am I lying in water? I consider opening my eyes. Dare I? The brilliance stabs my brain. I bring my arms up to my face and peer at them. It's difficult to focus.

There are ugly marks at the wrist, some healed, some still raw. They sting. I glimpse my legs. They're bare from the thighs down, white and latticed with cuts.

I close my eyes again and try to think. My memory lacks detail. In fact, I have no memory. I am…I can feel… But…

My body rocks gently. Waves splash over me, pushing me around.

I manage to drag myself a little out of the water. Despite the warmth, I'm shivering uncontrollably. Then I begin to retch. I spit out some briny water and something feels different. I try to move my tongue, to press it against my teeth to check… I have no tongue!

Sounds bombard me. I want to block out the noises; they're deafening. The crashing of waves, the shells and stones scraping together. I sense dark shapes up above in the brightness, mocking me with their fearful sounds of cackling and shrieking, and that piercing cry that builds to a scream. It emanates from my own throat.

Unidentified Man Found on Rangitoto

Auckland City Police are seeking the public's help to identify an elderly Caucasian man who was found in a distressed state, at the water's edge on the south-western side of Rangitoto island yesterday evening. He was discovered by a visiting group of tourists, who had spotted a body floating in the shallows.

The man is described as being emaciated and of indeterminate age, with long white hair and an unkempt beard. He has pale, fair, skin and grey eyes. The man, who was in a fragile state, was treated for hypothermia by the crew of the Westpac Rescue Helicopter, and then flown to North Shore Hospital's Intensive Care Unit. He is now in the critical care ward. He has been unable to provide an explanation of where he came from, nor were there any identifiable items on his person.

Frank's Story

My name is Francis Woodburn. My father died in the Great War when I was four. Mother was thirty when they got together—that was old for those times—and she never remarried. She had a sister who remained single, too. I guess there weren't so many men around after The War. My mother didn't really like to talk much about my father. When I was older she moved south, so I didn't see much of her up until she died. We wrote to each other—that's about all.

As an only child, I spent a lot of time by myself. When I grew older, I never really had a mind to marry anyone. Never felt the need.

Perhaps it's because Mother would never talk about it, but I've always had a 'thing' about the war, and about my father, too.

In 1955 I was living in the city, running a second-hand bookshop just off Mt Eden Road. I'd occasionally purchase house-lots of books; deceased estates, that kind of thing, in the hope that something valuable might turn up.

This story begins on a Tuesday morning. I'd just set up a display of gardening books in the front window when the phone rang. It was a gentleman I knew, who told me that his next-door neighbour had been found dead and that the family were at the house, sorting through her possessions.

"She was a nice old biddy, used to be married to some military chap, based over at North Head, I reckon there'd be some books in that house that might interest you."

So, I shut up shop for the morning, drove down to Onehunga and parked outside the address. It was an old wooden villa, quite fancy. I knocked on the door and made myself known to the sons. When they realised that I bought house-loads of books they perked up considerably. I had cash in my pocket (always pays to be prepared), a few quid changed hands and they led me to their father's study. The room was a mess with books all over the place. My heart sank. It was obvious someone had been through the shelves before me. My face must've displayed my disappointment as one of the sons chipped in,

"Yeah, sorry. Our sister's been here ahead of you, that's why I didn't think it'd hurt to take you up on your offer."

He looked like he had more to say, so I waited.

"People from the old man's work turned up, too. They carted away quite a bit of his personal material. Military stuff, and some 'souvenirs' they called them."

That'd teach me to think I'd won something over on the chap. I kept my face neutral.

"I see. You've had a generous deal from me, then."

I was glad that they left me to it and started packing the remaining books into the empty beer crates I'd brought for the purpose. They were mostly of little value, although I knew that I'd be able to on-sell some of the reference books.

I lifted a couple of encyclopaedias and saw that I'd exposed a thin volume, lying flat on the shelf beneath, well-hidden. I picked it up and carefully untied the ribbon that bound it. I walked to the window and peered closely at the inscription on the inside cover, 'Journal of Doctor Edgar McLeod, 1896'. Interesting.

I re-tied the bow and carefully placed it between the two encyclopaedias, then packed them in with the other books. When I arrived back at the shop, I spent the rest of the day unpacking my purchases and seeing to the needs of the few customers who came in. The journal was waiting for me on a table in the back room, and I was looking forward to examining it more closely.

Dr McLeod's Diary

When I finally had the chance, I held the volume before me and surveyed the covers. They were of dark green leather, stained with watermarks and beginning to scuff at the edges. Inside, the pages were closely written in a fine, slanting script. Many of the pages had dated headings, in the manner of a diary. In some places, the ink had quite faded. This would make them difficult to decipher. Additionally, within the pages, a number of folded hand-written diagrams and maps had been inserted, and these in particular were well-thumbed and worse for wear. About two-thirds through, the writing abruptly ceased. In fact, it appeared that McLeod had stopped writing mid-sentence. The remainder of the pages were blank.

I turned to the beginning of the document, and began to read…

"My name is Edgar James McLeod and I am putting pen to paper to record the sequence of strange and disturbing events that I have witnessed this year past.

"The league of which I am a member is comprised of one dozen upstanding citizens of the City of Auckland's community. Our purpose has been to seek and uncover knowledge not previously revealed to the common man. Through the guidance of our leader, we have made unimaginable progress. In fact, we have made the acquaintance of an ancient being, an Old Unnamed One.

"Beneath the military bunkers of North Head, there runs a vast system of tunnels, many of which have been requisitioned by the army. But there are other corridors, which wend their way far deeper, and beyond these there lies a series of ancient caverns. It is within these chambers that the Unnamed One resides."

McLeod's opening paragraphs drew me in immediately, how could they not?

Over the next several evenings, once I'd closed up shop for the day, I pored through his notes. The more I read, the more I became intrigued by his account.

McLeod wrote that the members of his secret society had individually been acquainted with each other in London, and had been recruited into the group upon arrival in Auckland. Their mentor and leader went by the unremarkable name of, 'the Major', suggesting a military background, and indeed, McLeod was careful to only refer to his fellow members by either their surname alone (i.e., Smith or Johnston), or by occupation, (e.g., 'the Politician', or 'the Italian').

His description of the Major, however, covered a complete paragraph. "He is lanky with an awkward gait, almost dragging one leg behind him. It has been said that he sustained an injury in The Crimean War and has a weeping ulcer, but I doubt this is true. However, there is a smell about him that no amount of Cologne can disguise. Men avoid his proximity and yet are also drawn to him. He has a way about him, and yet I do not care to catch his eye."

In the mid-1880s, North Head was under the control of the New Zealand Army, and the 'Major' was indeed associated with the military. This association allowed him to organise clandestine work below ground in conjunction with the bunkers and tunnels being built in anticipation of an expected Russian invasion. Convicts were used to extend the army's tunnels, and it seemed that at least two prison guards were paid by the society to steer work into other more secretive areas. McLeod didn't explain how the Major acquired his information, but from the outset, all his energies were focused on the construction of the concealed set of corridors.

As McLeod's account progressed, his tone changed from excitement, to reservation, to a strange uncertainty. He began to get lost in convoluted thought; his choice of words became cryptic (almost code-like) and his descriptions more obscure. The final entry was completely unsatisfactory, merely stating, "Tomorrow morning we shall know one way or the other. I am hoping that the Major will err on the side of common sense."

I was left feeling frustratingly short-changed.

North Head

When I was at college we all had to serve a stint as cadets. For a few weeks each year, we were billeted at North Head and underwent infantry training. I didn't mind—it was a diversion from regular schoolwork, and, as I said, the military side of things interested me. By day we were under tight control (the usual drills and gun practices) but at night no-one seemed to care what we got up to, as long as we didn't do anything that drew attention to ourselves. We just had to keep quiet and avoid trouble.

Some of us used to creep out of the dormitory after lights out, to explore the tunnels. We'd apply boot polish to our faces, don woollen hats and kit ourselves out with torches. Once away from the main tunnels, which were usually lit, one of the first things you'd notice was the complete and utter darkness—it wasn't the kind of place you'd wish to explore without a torch, that's for sure. The place was like a rabbit warren with winding tunnels leading deeper and deeper under the hill, and vertical vents that drew the eye upwards. The vents had metal rungs leading up into the darkness and if you shone your torch up, the beam just disappeared. Some of the tunnels were wide enough to drive a convoy of vehicles along, while others could merely be glimpsed through barred windows. There were dead ends with doors made of riveted steel, sporting huge padlocks. The place had an eerie feel to it, too. It was almost as if someone was watching us, just out of sight, but I'd always put that down to it being night-time and the excitement of being out of bounds.

McLeod's notes described something quite different. For one thing, he wrote about the original tunnel works, the sections built in the mid to late 1880s, when everything was newly constructed. Then he was writing about a complete network of secret tunnels that led deeper, straight down into the depths below North Head, straight to a series of vast subterranean caverns.

Although his writing was difficult to make sense of in places, I read on, and as I did so, I tried to match his descriptions to my own sketchy memories of the place. The key was in the location of one particular 'legitimate' tunnel that was also the entry point to the series of secret tunnels. According to his account, this tunnel lay directly behind a building he referred to as 'the laboratory'. The more I read, the more certain I was that this was the dwelling now known as the 'shepherd's cottage' situated on the southwestern face. If I was correct, then this entrance was the key to gaining access to the hidden sections.

For some days I'd had it in the back of my mind that I'd have to go and find these caverns of McLeod's, just to satisfy my own curiosity if nothing else. Though, if I'm to be honest, for the first time in my life I experienced a thrill of excitement.

North Head was hardly a security risk in the 1950s, but it was still under military control. I knew there'd most likely be a nightly picket, but still felt sure it would be easy to avoid anyone on duty and slip into the compound under the cover of darkness. Once inside, I was confident that I could follow the detailed descriptions and maps provided by McLeod.

As I made my plans I worked hard to suppress my excitement. I decided to make an initial test run to see if I could gain entry on the next clear, moonless night. In the meantime, I gathered together a small kit of items that I felt would be useful: a torch, spare batteries, a brass compass, a length of hessian rope, and a hunting knife. Finally, I had everything I needed, and I'd read the relevant sections of McLeod's text often enough to commit the pertinent details to memory. If the weather stayed settled, I would make my first attempt on the following Monday.

Beneath the Hill

I looked up at the brow of North Head, catching my breath. I clearly wasn't as fit as I used to be. Earlier, I'd parked in Devonport, about a half mile from the entrance gates, and made my way along Takarunga Road with purpose, as if I had every right to be visiting. The gates were locked to cars, but the side gate was open. Once within the grounds, and out of sight of the nearest houses, I ducked off the road and onto the grass verge. The muted sounds of the city were soon left behind, and the soft crunch of my boots on the grass formed a rhythm that reminded me of the military drills of twenty-five years earlier.

My route took me northwards initially, but after a hairpin turn to the right I was headed in a southerly direction. The wind was stronger on this side, but I welcomed the freshness of it. After about ten minutes I spied the shepherd's cottage, tucked into the hillside. The dim glow of a light showed behind one of the curtained windows, and as I watched, the shadow of a figure moved from one side of the room to the other. It hadn't occurred to me that the place would be occupied. However, I soon realised that it didn't really matter, as the swirling wind rattled and tore at the scrubby vegetation, its whistling sounds muffling the sounds of my approach.

The hill behind the cottage seemed to take on an ominous aspect and I thrust my right hand into the pocket of my jacket to feel the cool metal handle of my torch. Overhead, the last wintry clouds that had cast dampness on the city all day were scattering. Through them I could perceive the flicker of the first stars. They had a cold and spectral allure.

There was no point in lingering out in the open, so I made my way closer to the dwelling, behind which I could just make out the tunnel entrance as a darker shape in the slope. A narrow concrete path wound around the left side, but the single window was dark. In the lee of the building I could clearly hear the sound of a radio. I pictured the occupant sitting in the warmth, glad to be indoors on such a night.

Turning away from the cottage, I surveyed the entrance to the tunnel. The opening was barred with a pair of wrought iron gates hinged at floor and ceiling to sturdy metal plates set into the walls. A thick chain was looped through the centre of the gates, and to this a padlock had been attached, but the lock hadn't been closed. I carefully slid off both padlock and chain and placed them on the ground at my feet, then tested the gates. They swung inwards with barely a sound. I shone the torch at the hinges. They were freshly oiled and gleamed a little. I was grateful for the excitement in my chest, considering it a positive attribute, one that would carry me forth despite the unwelcoming aspect of the dank tunnel that lay beyond. Even so, my heart was pounding madly, and I had to take a moment to catch my breath and to slow my breathing down, before stepping over the threshold and pulling the gates closed behind me.

Gaining access to the first tunnel had almost been too easy. I decided to wait for a few moments to take stock of the situation, and to calm my breathing. A few drops of perspiration slithered down my back. The padlock and chain still lay on the ground at my feet and I considered re-attaching them, but I was hesitant. What if they somehow locked themselves? The thought of being locked in the tunnel and having to explain myself didn't appeal to me. In the end I decided to move them further into the passage, out of sight of the immediate area. I deemed it highly unlikely that anyone would check the entrance after nightfall, especially when it was positioned directly behind an occupied cottage. And if someone did, perhaps he'd just think someone had been slack about security.

Turning back towards the tunnel, the beam from my torch revealed a dry corridor, wide enough for three men to walk comfortably, side by side. The floor and walls were of white-washed concrete and there was a dusty, dry smell about the place. I could see the faint outlines of side exits and ceiling vents at the furthest point of the beam. The area appeared tidy, with only a few dried leaves underfoot, just inside the gates. According to McLeod I'd need to follow this first tunnel almost to the end, while counting the exits on the right-hand wall. The hidden entrance to the secret section was in a room accessed from the sixth exit on that side, which led directly into a storage room. He'd written that even at the time the tunnels were in regular use, the entrance was well-hidden within the room, and my primary aim that night was merely to locate this entrance. I had no plans of what I might do after this, as I had no idea of how long this exercise might take, or even if it would be successful.

The tunnel was in good shape and seemed to travel in a straight line, without deviation in either direction or slope. But even so, I walked with trepidation, shining my torch ahead and at the roof and walls as I walked. I was surprised to see that the smooth concrete floors remained surprisingly bereft of debris. Perhaps even now, this tunnel was being used for a military purpose of some kind. While I was only concerned with the exits to the right, there were also a number that branched off to the left. Some were open doorways, while others had metal doors, and the familiar metal grills that could be looked through. Shining my torch into one revealed a single room, with boxes stacked up in one corner.

It was cool in the tunnels and draughty—chilly air funnelled down through the ceiling vents and despite my warm clothing I began to notice the reduction in temperature. However, after a relatively short time, I came upon the sixth exit. This egress had an actual door, although it had been broken half off its hinges and one edge was now wedged into the floor. I pushed my way through, shining the torch tentatively in all directions. Inside the room, the concrete floor was broken in several places, which made the surface somewhat difficult to walk on. I shone my torch on the cracks. The ground underneath (what I could see of it) looked soft and boggy.

The room was rectangular, about four yards by three, with no other obvious exits. Directly to my left was a grey metal desk. I laid the torch on its surface so that the beam illuminated the room as best as possible and looked around carefully. This had originally been a storage room but had clearly fallen into disrepair; not just the wrecked floor but also the furnishings looked as if they'd been knocked around. There may even have been a fire in the room at some point, if the black ashen mass under the metal desk was anything to go by.

Something about the room made me uncertain. I couldn't exactly put my finger on the cause, but I decided to proceed with caution. I stood completely still and quietened my breathing but could hear nothing. All but one wall had stacks of shelves and these were empty of contents. In the far-left corner directly facing me, a panelled wooden storage unit was built into the wall. It ran from floor to ceiling and had a full-length door on one side, and rows of drawers on the other. I picked up my torch and walked carefully across to the cupboard. The sight of the cabinet reassured me that I was in the correct room; it matched McLeod's description exactly. Hopefully it would provide access to the hidden section.

There didn't appear to be any obvious way of opening it, but I knew that this wasn't the case. Stretching upwards I felt along the top of the unit until I came upon a small depression, which I pressed firmly. I heard a faint click from within the cabinet and the door swung open the merest crack. Success! At that very moment my torch flickered and went out. I pressed the switch off and on a few times to no avail, and in my confusion, I dropped it at my feet. Reaching down, I managed to retrieve it, but for a moment I felt as if I was unable to breathe.

The spare batteries were in my pocket and I fumbled in the pitch darkness to replace the spent ones with the new ones. The intense blackness seemed to have a presence of its own. I imagined an inky vapour oozing its way beneath my clothes, its shadowy fingers probing against my chest and moving past my breastbone towards my throat. I shook the feeling off, regained my composure and concentrated on finishing the task. I was glad when my torch shone brightly again and aimed it towards the inside of the cupboard. The back of the enclosure was also of dark panelled wood. There was a row of brass coat hooks, one of which had an ancient gas mask hanging from it.

I couldn't see any way of opening that back panel, even though I knew that it could move aside. I began to feel frustrated, thinking back to what McLeod had written. His notes had merely said, 'the secret area is accessed through the cabinet'. I shone my torch around the rectangular space once again, and then noticed that the fourth brass hook looked subtly different from the others. As I reached up to touch it, I noticed my hand was shaking, and reminded myself of the benefits of breathing slowly and evenly. It only took the slightest of touches and the panel slid to the side with almost no sound. The dank smell I'd noticed on and off all evening surrounded me as if in a cloud, then dissipated. I coughed, and the sound seemed to echo a long way into the distance.

I stepped back and took stock. I'd achieved the target I'd set myself for the night. Not only had I easily found the access room, I'd also successfully gained entrance to McLeod's hidden area. I was already on to my spare set of batteries and I was tired and cold. The tension of the exploration had definitely taken its toll on my energy levels. And that moment of complete blackness a few minutes ago had disturbed me more than it should have. Perhaps it was time to head back home. Who knew what lay beyond this room? But, I was curious. To have come so far in so short a time, surely it wouldn't hurt to investigate just a little further?

The Caverns of the Unnamed One

Beyond the secret entrance was another tunnel and I was surprised to find that after a few yards, it had a noticeable downhill gradient. It was also clearly curving to the left, bringing it closer to the heart of the headland. My nostrils twitched at the odour of mossy wetness, which almost covered the unpleasant smell I'd been noting on and off all evening. And there was the sensation of a deep and penetrating cold that seemed to rise up out of the darkness. Somewhere not too distant I could just make out the sound of water dripping; it had an almost melodic quality and I wondered how long it had been since other feet had trod the same path or heard the same sounds. My torch shone strongly, and its beam illuminated not only the path before me, but also the walls and ceiling. From time to time, rectangular air vents broke the roof. I stopped to shine the torch up into the first two or three I came upon, but could see nothing of interest. Even the metal rungs on the vents of the more recent tunnels were not in evidence here. But the air seemed fresh enough. And yet I could not dispel the feeling that I was being watched. Impossible, of course, but even so…

According to McLeod's account, the main tunnel, the one through which I was now walking, proceeded for fifty yards, at which point I should encounter a crossroads. Turning right would take me directly to a small bay on the southwestern side of the headland. A left-hand turn would take me to a chamber he referred to as the 'preparation' room. Preparation for what, I could not imagine.

My plan had originally been to keep going straight ahead, as, according to McLeod, a few yards further in this direction would lead me directly to the 'meeting room'—the chamber in which the group initially made contact with the 'Unnamed One'. His account left out more than it explained, but there was no denying the underlying expectation he'd built up. However, when I reached this intersection I could see no reason not to turn left to have a quick look at the preparation room. The metal door to this room, while still intact, was hinged back against the passageway wall, bolted to an iron clasp. It was one of the types of doors that had a barred, glass-less window around head height. I peered through the doorway.

The chamber was spacious; about ten yards square. My stomach lurched when I realised that the room had clearly once been used to confine living beings, for fixed into the concrete walls were sets of manacles, at both ankle and shoulder height. There were a couple of rude bunks, upon which could still be seen the remains of army-style mattresses, although these were clearly ancient, stuffed as they were with straw (I could see the stalks clearly through a mattress that had fallen foul to rodents). The floor of the chamber was of hard-packed earth, and around its perimeter ran a shallow trough that led to a drain in one corner. The place smelled rank, perhaps due to the damp patches on the floor upon which an unbecoming slime had accumulated. This led me to believe that the location was closer to sea level than I'd expected. I remained motionless for a moment, surveying the scene, and for the first time, I felt some misgivings about the purpose of the supposed coven McLeod had been involved with.

A heavy weariness began to overcome me. It was as if the very task of lifting my feet had become inordinately difficult. The smell was also beginning to have an effect, causing me to feel quite nauseous. Perhaps I'd dwelt too long in the subterranean passages. The allure of fresh air and sparkling stars suddenly became overwhelmingly attractive. I decided to explore no further on that night. I'd successfully found the first chamber. It only followed that the main chamber would also be discoverable. I'd retrace my steps and head home.

I leaned back against the inner wall of the chamber to gather my breath, switching off my torch to save the batteries; relieved that the visions of the living vapour weren't intruding this time. The darkness was complete; not a glimmer of light could be seen. My thoughts were in disarray and I kept thinking back to the sight of the manacles. Could McLeod's coven have had a darker purpose?

My reveries were interrupted by a noise emanating from further along the passage, causing me to stand up straight, straining my ears. It was as if a heavy object was being dragged along the ground. After a few moments I realised that the sound was drawing closer. My mind raced. For what purpose would someone else be down this far below the hill, at such a time? Glancing towards the entrance, I fancied that the corridor outside was growing lighter, and yes, I could soon see the silhouette of the doorway. Beyond it was a strange luminosity, greenish and flickering. The hairs rose on the back of my neck and I stood there bathed in uncertainty. Should I keep still in the hope that the originator of the noise kept on going, or should I turn on my torch (thus exposing myself) in the hope that I could make a run for it? In my fear I had convinced myself that whoever or whatever was making its way towards the chamber was not a living man, and therefore I was unlikely to be able to explain myself out of the situation.

The sound drew ever closer, until, to my horror it came to a halt directly outside. A malodorous stench began to fill the room. Then the muffled scraping started up again. The torch was still gripped in my right hand, and, drawing on all the courage I could muster, I stepped into the outside tunnel and raised it high above my shoulder. Simultaneously, I pressed the switch and shone the beam directly at the shuffling noise.

At first, I could make no sense of what I was seeing. And

yet my brain tried to find words for the vision before me. A corpulent whitish shape, far taller and wider than any creature I was familiar with, rippling with an oily slick of green slime, filled almost all the space available in the tunnel. At its head squirmed a mass of tentacles and these were twitching and wriggling predatorily. Behind these I glimpsed a spheroid pair of gleaming yellow eyes. These were fixed on me, revealing a glacial and malignant intelligence.

The sight was so alien, and so fearsome that the torch fell from my slack grip and I turned to run, panic rising in my throat. But I wasn't quick enough. One of the thing's tentacles shot out and gripped me by the waist. Another tightened around my throat. I lost consciousness.

When I awoke that first time, it was as if I'd descended into hell. But there was no fire in those ghastly depths. To burn would have been a sweet death in comparison.

My captor would visit me frequently in the first few days, which soon ran into weeks, then months. Long before then I had stopped considering time in units. I just was. The realisation that I was to be kept alive, in itself, was a kind of death.

These are my memories. They come to me under cover of darkness, when I lie unconscious on my hospital bed. I relive these moments over and over, and yet I know that when I awaken, these dreams will be fleeting wisps of imagination, unable to be grasped or explained.

Epilogue

Dr Richardson looked up as the door to his office opened. He gestured towards the seat in front of his desk. His visitor sat down.

"Thanks for taking the time to update me on our mystery

man. I take it he still hasn't communicated anything?"

"Not yet, no," said Richardson, drily. "Have you had any luck with working out where he came from?"

"No. To be honest, we have no leads. I'm thinking he'll remain a mystery. You said you had some additional information relating to his injuries?"

"Yes. It seems this isn't just a case of some old guy falling off a boat and being washed ashore. He has a range of long-term repetitive injuries that he'd clearly sustained long before he ended up in the water."

The police inspector's eyes narrowed, but he said nothing as Richardson continued.

"Did you see him when he was first admitted to hospital?"

"Yes, I was on duty that night. I arrived here a few minutes before they brought him in," the Inspector replied.

"And did you notice anything unusual about him?"

"Well, his appearance, the long, straggly hair and beard, and his clothes. They were old-fashioned, and pretty much in tatters. And I did notice that his legs were badly scratched, but I thought that was just from the rocks." He paused for a moment.

"I hear his tongue is missing… How do you think that happened?"

"Hard to say, exactly, but it looks like it may have been pulled out."

The Inspector grimaced.

"And when I assessed the patient, I found evidence of old injuries long healed, as well as the obvious, more recent injuries. His wrists and ankles are badly scored with scars and festering flesh—it's as if he's been bound at both ankles and wrists on and off for very long periods of time. Then there are the nails on his toes and fingers, the ones he still has," Richardson looked up, "They were so long it would've been extremely difficult to use his hands or to walk. We've cleaned them up, of course, but his hands are virtually useless."

The two men sat in silence for a moment.

"I did notice his eyes. He seemed to look right through me, and the way he stared wasn't natural. It was as if he wasn't all there, if you know what I mean. Or as if he's seen things he can't talk about", the inspector's voice faded a little, "And you say he's said nothing at all?"

"Just incoherent mumblings. It's almost like he's trying to say one particular word, but without a tongue, it's hard to be sure."

The inspector shifted on his chair and stood to leave, "Well, thanks for this. Like I said. We don't really have any leads. So not sure who we could charge over your suspicions." He turned towards the door, and then looked back at Richardson. "It seems obvious he's been held prisoner somewhere for years, but where? Where's he been washed up from?"

The doctor shook his head, "He can't talk, can barely communicate. Doesn't seem to like looking at anyone. He's more likely to close his eyes than to communicate. It's a shame, though. Someone should be held responsible, and he'd have quite a story to tell, if only he could." Richardson closed the file on his desk and nodded farewell to the inspector, who stopped in the doorway and looked back.

"What will happen to him if he does survive?"

"Well…if he makes it through the first couple of weeks and we can stabilise him, I think I know of a place that might care for him." Richardson's face took on a speculative air. "There's a private facility…coincidentally, it's directly across from where he was found. Been running for years."

"Oh? And you think they'd take him?"

"I think so. It's a hospital-come-residential home that was set up decades ago using a bequest from an eccentric old guy known as 'the Major'.

KŌPURA RISING

DAVID KURARIA

1

It is strange how investigation into one area of research can reveal a path to another, a path that sends a normal life full of stability and sameness spiralling into a frightening unknown. Tales are numerous where simple adventure leads to peril.

For some months I had been saving for a trip to the Solomon Islands, in Melanesia, to further my studies in marine reptile toxicology. A colleague, Rita Phillips, showed me maps of the islands and during our free time we researched a little about the history of the area. During my summer break I boarded a flight from Auckland, north to the Solomons' capital, Honiara.

Rita drove me out to the airport in South Auckland to catch my flight. As I left her, she handed me a few pages of text she had downloaded.

"Here, Lomu, a little something for you to read on the plane. It's about a missing Norwegian anthropologist."

I took the stapled sheets and flicked through.

"Is this another one of your conspiracy mysteries of lost explorers?"

"Yep," she said with a grin. "It's a travel diary from one Tors Haugen, disappeared out in the Arctic Ocean in 1999. These are copies of notes found in his apartment, prior to his last expedition, when he and eight members of his team went missing. The notes are strange, to say the least."

I remember being thankful, mainly because there were not

too many pages to read. I folded the sheets and put them into my shirt pocket.

Once airborne and out over the Pacific I took the pages from my pocket and folded them flat. Over the peeps and gongs from the aircraft and overheard snippets of conversations from nearby passengers, I began reading.

Tors Haugen, meteorologen,
January 15 1999, Skara Brea, Orkney, Scotland.

For nearly two years now, I have found myself fascinated by tales of a legendary race of ocean dwellers. I have been researching folklore, fireside tales passed from Britain's Outer Hebrides in the eighteenth century, up through the Arctic Ocean from the Orkney Islands to Greenland—tales of creatures named 'Kvakeri: the hidden people of the sea'. Whenever temporarily stationed in the Arctic Ocean I have used free time outside official capacity to speak to island locals of myths and legends. In the Hebrides, I was told tales by local fishermen about 'Blue Men of the Minch'. In the Orkney Islands oral traditions from farmers told of salt lickers, wild tales from leather-faced, grim men with little sense of humour.

Late summer 1999 I was gathering data on North Atlantic weather patterns for a report that was due. While in Tórshavn, in the Faroe Island, I sought out people to try and find variants on tales I had been told. Over the years I have realised the best place to hear stories is at local inns. It was in Tórshavn where I first heard the name 'Kvakeri'.

Fishermen say Kvakeri can take many forms, are able to alter shape and colour. These are repulsive tales where Kvakeri are alleged to feed on the flesh of drowned fishermen—placing mouths against the dead, swallowing salt by licking skin, the creatures' sandpaper tongues stripping flesh from bone.

I held the notes on my lap and looked about the cabin of the aircraft. I felt a little ill at the disgusting suggestion of licking a dead person's flesh. I stared at the headrest of the seat in front of me for a moment, to gather my thoughts. Then I looked down again at the pages in my lap and, against my better judgement, began reading the Norwegian's next diary entry.

Tors Haugen, meteorologen,
January 17 1999, Arctic Ocean.

While in Tórshavn I paid my passage on a local fishing boat to a coastal village on an outer island. I found an inn and introduced myself to a small group of locals at a table. Their dialect was a strange hybrid but I did my best to speak and understand it, and a few drinks of fine Danish Vodka later the three men were willing to answer my questions. These weather-beaten tars soon provided new slants on what I already knew; added colour, finished one-another's sentences. The oldest, seeming to be in his eighties, had not actually seen these cryptids, but heard terrifying tales when just a boy. He related to me how the skin of the Kvakeri shifted across itself during sunny days, as if muscles underneath were changing shape.

I remained with these men for nearly half an hour and was told gruesome stories of bloodlust and terror brought to lone fishermen who had strayed too far from shore. I can state here, without doubt, that these men, with their tales of horror, seemed to be enjoying themselves.

At the end of our conversation I realised that, of all the differing accounts of crypto-marine predators I had gathered over the past two years, it was most likely I was hearing about the same creatures.

On my way back to Tórshavn I spoke with another sailor on the boat ferrying me, who told me of Kvakeri supposedly living north of the Russian mainland in the Laptev Sea.

2

Honiara was a bit of a shock to the system after having been at Manukau Airport only some six hours before. Outside the bustling terminal were market stalls and local taxis, their windows smudged with insects. I went back into the terminal to escape the humidity and asked about getting out to Bina Lagoon on north-west Mwaia, the largest and most populous island of the eastern chain. I was told to speak to someone at the docks in regard to buying a ticket for the inter-island supply boat, Echo.

I booked into a backpacker hostel and dropped my bag in my room. I bought a little guidebook and ate at a nearby outdoor café. While there I learned some local Kirabati words I thought would help me fit in. Afterwards I found the waterfront police station and went inside, glad to escape the humidity, and stood for a few seconds under a ceiling fan. I approached two officers talking and waited for them to notice me. They turned and stared. I realised they knew I was not a local. They approached and the shorter man smiled and slowly shook his head.

"Don't tell me, you've had your wallet stolen, right?"

"Oh, no. I want to go out to Mwaia and I was wondering if you might know who I could speak to about finding sea snakes. The officers looked at me, then turned to each other. They grinned. Both said at the same time, "Renai." One of them laughed.

"Yes, big fellow, curly blonde Mwain, ripped clothes. Ask anyone for Renai."

Echo was a diesel run deep keel, close to thirty-metres long, with old-world touches such as dark wood panelling on the interior of the main cabin. The trip across to Mwaia was quite rough, as the stretches of water between the islands were really open sea. There were only a handful of other passengers on board. In the centre of the enclosed cabin was a wired enclosure opened at the top at waist height. Inside were stuffed sacks and cartons, which I guessed were supplies for the outlying communities.

It was not too long before we arrived at Mwaia, an enormous green, lofty expanse of jungle and dark rock. I looked up past the valleys and crags and saw that the highest peaks were shrouded in mist. The captain slowed *Echo*, chugged parallel to the beach and tooted the whistle. He manoeuvred the craft to lie next to a dilapidated jetty, where his crewmen secured the vessel and unloaded some cargo. Some waiting residents of the nearby village, visible beyond a rocky promontory, began loading the cargo onto big-wheeled, wooden, flat carts. I was ignored until I got the attention of one burly man.

"I'm looking for Renai."

He grinned and pointed out into the lagoon. I saw many small islets in the shallow expanse of clear water. Locals were toiling with large rocks and seemed to be building sea walls. I lifted my one bag onto my shoulder, waded out into the lagoon, and made my way towards the nearest of the islets.

As I approached I saw it was actually a platform of excavated coral with a soil covered top, about twenty by thirty metres. A hut built from bamboo with a woven palm leaved roof was set upon packed topsoil. I waded out of the clear water up onto a sloping beach of sand.

The sun was still rising behind the massive bulk of Mwaia. On another islet was a big man with a thick matt of curly blonde hair. I watched as he hefted a large piece of coral he had pried with a machete from the bottom of the lagoon. He was helping other men build a platform much like the islet I was standing upon.

One of the men looked in my direction. He pointed at me and said something to the blonde-haired man, who turned and stared at me. He grinned and waved. I knew I had found Renai. He waded across the lagoon and walked up onto the beach. He looked at the big island filling the foreground, stretched his arms wide and spoke.

"Ahhh, Mwaia, my strange Melanesian beauty—you are one of the last true oddities on a shrinking planet. Lomu Morgan, aren't you? Jeez, lad, with your skin you'll be hard to tell from us locals. So it is sea snakes you are after?"

"That's me—just in from Auckland. But how did…?"

"I heard you were shipping out from Honiara. Cops texted me." He walked up to the thatched enclosure. "This is my place. I have the only freezer around these parts."

He must have seen my confused gaze. He gave a booming laugh.

"You as well? Oh, I can see that look. How does this Solomon Island man speak such good English? We all do, and our mothers and fathers and grandparents do, too. We have done since the Americans were here during the Pacific War. When you're bartering with the person who has the most goodies, you soon learn to understand what they are saying. Now that's out of the way, what say we sit and relax, okay?"

I was a little dazed at the quickness of it all, but I followed Renai into the hut.

He took two tins of orange fizzy drink from the icebox he called a freezer. He pointed to the seating arrangement. There were old car seats, still sitting on their metal pipe bases, placed under the thatch roof. I sat on one. Renai handed me a can of drink. He looked out at the lagoon.

"I'll speak to some of the elders about helping you with catching sea snakes, but you won't get anyone to help you today or tomorrow. People here need time to think things over."

I looked at him. "Thank you for helping me out, I appreciate it. I'm going to fit into your schedule as best I can. I researched a bit before I came. The sea level is rising in this part of the world. I guess that's why you're building these coral platforms."

Renai stared at me. "If someone measures that the sea has crept a little higher on a rock face, well, who is to say the islands are not sinking? Anyway, stuff about building coral platforms for rising tides is only half truth."

I had to ask. "What do you mean?"

Renai looked out across the lagoon. The intensity of that look made me uncomfortable. He pointed at the great island of Mwaia. "These people, my family, are suffering an old problem with upland Kwaio who won't let us share and farm their roaming place." Renai again pointed to the looming mass of the island. "Mwaia is not what it seems."

"In what way?"

"Well, during the battles here last century, American soldiers disappeared up there."

"Disappeared?"

"Patrols were sent to find Japanese outposts on the Beast; the patrols didn't return. Other patrols were sent after the missing soldiers. They were never found."

"So the search patrols came back empty handed. No clues?"

"No, I mean the search patrols never came back."

It was easy to believe soldiers could fall into hidden caves or get murdered by locals, especially back in 1942, when there were no cell phones or social media, and there was a war going on. If the soldier carrying the one radio fell down a crevasse, well, that was communication gone. Renai cut into my thoughts.

"A fern grows here, with tiny leaves that mesh thick, and covers holes, so unwary people fall down open cave mouths, and when the fern springs back into place, all traces are lost. Even if you looked you would see nothing but spongy moss. Step in the wrong place and down you go, not a trace. There are World War Two rifles and water canteens and belt buckles hidden down holes, and in caves, all across The Beast, with skeletons right up alongside"

"What do you mean by 'The Beast'?"

"It is a living thing, Mwaia, not friendly to some." He pointed at the towering mass of the island. "Upland Kwaio own the coastlands on this east side, and all the sands. Their spies, the shore people, work the croplands here and stop us from getting the good earth to feed ourselves. They say their roaming place is Tambu to others, and they enforce it. I've seen my friends speared and threatened with machetes, and so we have to feed ourselves with fish and taros. The only reason anything actually grows on our garden lots is because we risk attack by sneaking ashore to get buckets of dirt." Renai turned in his chair and watched his friends wading in the lagoon, then turned back to me.

"I'm going be gone for a while, talk to some people. When I come back we can fix a place for you to sleep for the next few days. There's some dried fish under netting on those racks, and some fruit in the cool box over there."

I watched him wade out into the lagoon to his friends now shading themselves under the palm thatch roof of the living quarters on another of their constructed islets. With nothing else to do but wait, I grabbed a bottle of water from the icebox and sat on a car seat. It was a good time to finish reading about the Norwegian explorer.

Tors Haugen, February 3rd, 1999,
Stavangar, Norge.

Back here at my office in Stavangar. I have just been informed by a colleague that a Russian climate expedition from Moscow University is missing somewhere on the arctic Severnaya Islands. The Severnaya group is in the Laptev Sea, and I am reminded of the old sailor in the Faroe Islands, and what he told me about the Arctic Sea north of the Russian mainland.

I had not even had time to settle back into my lodgings and properly unpack from my Faroe trip when I got the phone call. Now I have been instructed to join a group of experts, a well-equipped joint Russian Norwegian team including meteorologists and geologists, in order to locate the first expedition. For the first time since beginning my research into the Kvakeri legend, I am feeling uneasy. The rescue expedition with guides has been set up and tomorrow I set off by air to the Arctic wilderness.

Tors Haugen, February 6th 1999,
Tamyr Severnaya, Laptev Sea.

Four month twilight of Arctic—red and purple cloud cover. Tamyr Severnaya landmass black and grey, uninviting, frightening. I am with a rescue party on lowlands looking at the forbidding mountain range. My team has argued about which is the safest route up the massif to the entrance of the cave system. My colleagues are not immune to concocting pointless mysteries better left to lay people. I feel trepidation at the thought of entering the caverns.

I wish these notes to remain in the care of my research collaborator and mentor, Anna Markesson. Anna is leaving us here at the Massif and returning to Stavangar. She has agreed to collect my diaries and research notes for safe keeping until my return.

I turned the page over to look for further diary entries, but there were no more. I dropped the pages next to me, stood and stepped from under the thatch. The mist had dispersed and the imposing peaks of Mwaia were now in view. It looked impressive, even a little scary. I thought of the soldiers who had disappeared there, as if the island had eaten them whole.

Eventually, Renai came back and fell into a seat. "I've organised for you to see a couple of people tomorrow. You're welcome to take a car seat here when you bed down."

"Thanks, I'm grateful."

I saw him pointing at the notes I had read. "What's that?"

"Just some old diary entries by a Scandinavian explorer. He disappeared up in the Arctic Ocean in the late 90s."

"May I read it?"

"Sure."

I left Renai to read while I circled the islet and studied the lagoon. The clear, shallow water was full of coral and bright coloured fish, in stark contrast to the green jungled bulk of Mwaia that dominated the skyline. I walked back to Renai's hut. He held the papers out to me.

"Interesting. We have our own tales…"

I sat opposite on one of the car seats. "Really? Like the Kvakeri?

"I've heard stories since I was a boy. Remember I told you about upland Kwaio? Well, there has always been talk of these others, living close by to the Kwaio. It's said these others have powers. As kids we were told these people could call bad weather and make people see things, do bad things, turn people to do harm to others."

"What, bogey-men? All countries have legends. You're educated, Renai. Come on now. This is the modern world." I pointed to the looming landmass. "This place is so densely populated."

"Don't let that fool you. Get up in those mountains, among the Kwaio, it's a whole other world. They have strange rules and customs."

I saw he was serious. "And you say they know of another tribe which live up there with them."

"I did not stay with them, more like near them, in some way—near, but far."

I did not even want to try to make sense of that.

"So, who are these other people?"

"Not people. They call them Ramo, but there are other names for them too."

I sat forward. He continued.

"It's said that the upland Kwaio 'disappear' people to the Ramo for who knows what reason. And it's true that every year people here in the Solomons disappear, not only locals. Last year three Australian scientists vanished out west of Ranongga."

I felt he was now back in the real world and decided to pursue the matter. "Were they never found?"

"No bodies were found, but the runabout they had hired from the Australian Navy on Gizo was found on a beach near their campsite, with all their diving equipment still on board. There was talk, but things quickly quietened down. The people out on Gizo stopped the search some two weeks in—nothing."

He stopped and stared at the dirt floor between his feet. I thought about what he said and looked out at the mountainous bulk of Mwaia. Renai slapped his knees.

"If you're keen on this kind of stuff, I have a story about a time I was working on a cable repair ship up near Guam."

I guess my eagerness was showing. Renai grinned, then I saw his demeanour change. He stared at his feet and when he raised his head he had become serious. I could see he was wrestling with some thought that troubled him.

3

Renai's Story

A few years ago I had a job as a crane operator on a fibre-optic cable repair ship. This was in the Mariana Islands up near Guam, you know, the American military own it. The ship was a big girl called the *Sumatra Queen*, captained by a fellow named Bennett, an angry man with an ulcer.

There had been a build-up of sediment on a submarine seamount and a small section had sheared away, causing a minor landslide, which damaged an optics cable. There were four of us manning the section at the stern that included the hoists and motors which ran the little ROV, or Remote Operating Vehicle, which is a fancy name for a small deep-sea submersible. A big gangly guy, Fulcrum, was my assistant, working the engine that ran the sub, along with another guy, Hodgson, who was monitoring depth and pressure. I was up on the crane. Our job was to keep the sub safe and bring up the fibre optic cable in its retractable claw. Marina Eyles, our IT technician, was the computer whiz operating the ROV from a room on the bulwark.

Off the side of this seamount there had been another minor slide next to the submersible. The slide had caused a swell and had swung the sub sideways so it had smacked up against the side of the undersea mountain. I had felt the movement up through the safety cable and had switched my engine to idle, so I could hear any orders Hodgson might have for me. He tapped his headphones and he looked up at me.

"What the hell was that?"

I leaned out and looked down at him.

"What was what?"

"That ringing sound. It's not the sub. It sounded hollow, almost as if the sub had hit something hollow."

I looked down and he waved his hand.

"Marina wants to raise the sub, but leave the cable behind. Bring it up, before there's another slide. Here, I'll patch her through"

Marina spoke to me through my headphones. "It all looks good, but I've let the cable go. Raise the ROV."

All through this I knew Bennett and the mate were monitoring the situation and were also in radio contact with Marina. I heard Hodgson through my headphones.

"We have a visitor."

I was not sure I heard right so I concentrated on getting the sub back up on deck. Seawater was still pouring off the little craft when I noticed something big wrapped around the ROVs grappling arm. It took me a few seconds to realise it was an animal. I remember staring at this odd looking thing and realising it had been hauled up from the sea floor. I thought about why it had not burst. Usually deep-sea creatures collapse and burst like popping bladders when they reach the surface. This was different. There was not even a wrinkling of the flesh. The thing was weird looking and wriggling so it was hard to see its true shape. It was blue grey with black splotches across a rounded head. It began squirming and squeaking and hissing like a tea-kettle, and it clung to the arm of the submersible as if it was its mother. Then it unwound. Next moment it was lying on the deck on its back thrashing and squealing. I couldn't get a good look at the thing because it was moving quickly and spinning over onto its stomach and again onto its back, jerking its head and screaming, but I know I saw something with legs or arms, lean and muscled. It was changing colour, from grey to pink to deep blue; it flopped across the deck and I saw a crest growing around its face, which looked like webbed spines. Its eyes were deep set and blood pressed from the edges.

Fulcrum leaned in for a closer look at this thing. He had a length of pipe and he prodded the beast. Without warning the thing opened its mouth and a stream of liquid spurted out into Fulcrum's face. He dropped the pole and began clawing at his eyes. I saw steam rising from his head and I knew the spew was hot. Fulcrum fell to the deck right next to the sea creature and started yelling out and cursing, all the time trying to wipe the stuff off his face. "Help me!"

I climbed down from the cab of the crane and jumped onto the deck. I saw the skin on Fulcrum's face had started to bubble. I remember looking at the thrashing sea creature and saw large pieces of scaly skin were peeling off, almost as if it was ill. I remember standing stupidly not really knowing what to do. Shouts sounded behind me and I heard boots clomping along the overhead companionway. The mate boomed an order.

"Someone get that idiot up off the deck. You, Hodgson, drop a tarpaulin over that screaming fish. Price, get the Doc and tell him to bring a cocktail syringe, move!"

I heard the mate behind me barking more orders, but only vaguely, because most of my concentration was centred on the squalling thing on the deck. I saw Fulcrum struggling to get away from the thing. I began to gag from the smell. The mate yelled at me.

"Renai, you useless shit, help the man."

I ran to get Fulcrum away from the thrashing creature. He was still clawing his fingers across his face. As I pulled him away I saw the creature's mouth gape wide. A wet, bulging sac was disgorged from its throat. I turned away and concentrated on helping drag Fulcrum to safety. The tarpaulin came down over the creature. I felt the mate's hand on my shoulder.

"Renai, let's go see the boss."

I hardly remember climbing up to the bridge. I sat for some time in a wardroom with Marina and Hodgson; Fulcrum had been whisked off to the medic. The next thing I was receiving orders to leave the ship. I was standing portside with the others watching a Guam Coast Guard cutter, *Pawtuxet,* parallel to the *Sumatra Queen*. A zodiac was sent over to pick us up to take us aboard the *Pawtuxet*. We weren't even allowed to grab our gear—that was sent along later and given back to us by some military cops. And they had gone through our stuff.

It was Marina who said it first. We had seen some kind of deep sea unknown, with which the navy was familiar. We were told to shut up. I knew it was not like some friend in the schoolyard saying: "Hey, you have to keep this a secret." We knew 'requests' from military personnel were definitely not requests.

We were taken back to Guam. Marina was assertive with the upper-echelon crew, but they were clearly under orders to ignore all our questions and demands. Marina was furious. When we berthed at a Guam naval base, we were taken under guard in the back of a transport vehicle through the town. After a few minutes, we were ordered into a one-storey building with a black glass front. Inside we were under guard. Two uniformed marines escorted us along a wide corridor. The guards were uncomfortable at Marina's aggressive attitude. They had let go of her arms and one of them walked alongside her, guiding her where he wished her to go. I could see they were a little afraid of her. With me the second marine was not so kind. He roughly pushed me along in front. At one point during our walk a massive door slid open. I saw an elevator about four metres wide. Inside was cavernous and looked as if it could hold a big vehicle. I had thought it odd for a one-storey building. We were escorted into a space that looked like a hospital waiting room with a row of chairs along one wall. We sat. The guards took Hodgson out of the room and locked the door behind them. We never saw him again. Guards came and took Marina away and I was alone for three hours.

A different person came and threw my passport and bag onto the floor. I saw my clothes and papers had been roughly stuffed back in. Before I could vent my anger, two other men came into the room. One was a sharply dressed man whom I guessed to be a civilian; the other was uniformed with rows of ribbons and medals on his jacket. He handed me a sheet of paper with a lot of text. His voice was unfriendly.

"Read and sign."

I wanted to get out of there, so I read the entire page as quick as I could. It basically stated I had voluntarily resigned my services aboard the *Sumatra Queen*. What made me sign the document so readily was when I read the attached names of my family and close friends. I knew a warning when I saw one. I realised this was in regard to the animal on our cable ship.

Ten minutes later, I was back in a military truck. I wondered where the others had been taken. With two Marines in the back with me, we had said nothing as we were driven to Wom Pat airport. There, I was met by another officer and provided with an air ticket to Honiara. I was left in the airport terminal, now desperate to get off Guam.

I sat on a bench, watching people. It was about an hour into my wait when a woman sat down next to me. I glanced at her and she spoke.

"Renai? Don't look at me. Just listen. I'm Lorraine. I'm a civilian research scientist, ichthyology. I'm going to leave a thumb drive on the seat next to you. I want you to take it and catch your plane. Look at what is on it when you are safe. There is an underground level called Nightmare Hall, which you need to see. It's all on the drive. I'm going to leave now. If you spot someone coming to question you, lift your hand and pretend to cough. Slip this in your mouth, between your teeth and your cheek."

She stood and walked away.

I lowered my hand and covered the drive. It was a tiny red plastic triangle. I gathered it up and held it, now feeling paranoid about being watched.

4

His story complete, Renai sat back and waited for my reaction. I had so many questions I didn't know where to start. I stood and peered out from under the thatch roof of the hut. Mwaia stretched to both horizons.

"I'll tell you what really scared me, Lomu. When I got off Guam and arrived home here, I checked some news feeds. I read that a research scientist had been found dead from a suspected drug overdose in a hotel room in Guam. I knew who it was."

I wondered briefly if I was being played, but my curiosity took control.

"So what was that thing on the cable ship?"

"I think I met one of the Ramo that day. Around here they call them Kõpura."

"You really believe this stuff—about this, um, Kõpura?"

"Didn't you hear what I said? I saw one and I'll never forget it. Add in what Lorraine told me—and I believe her—then they're here, right enough, living on The Beast. There are many names for them. 'Aporok' over in West Papua and 'Kõpura' hereabouts, and your Norwegian explorer mentions 'Kvakeri'. I think they could all be the same thing."

Renai leaned down and reached under the car seat next to him. He pulled out a crumpled shoebox, then rummaged inside.

"My life, it's all in here and here," he said, tapping his head. "Two memories, one in my head and one…here." He opened his hand and I saw a small plastic triangle.

"The thumb drive?"

"You can insert it into a phone if you have a late model, but your pad will do. The pop-up will tell you there are no files. What it does, instead, is divert files to a D drive that you can only access from your settings menu."

"There's stuff on there I should see, right?"

"Well, only if you want proof," Renai went to the icebox and took out a bottle of soda. "I've seen what's on this disk, and I don't need to see it again. I just want your opinion. I'm off to see some builders. I'll be back later." Without further word he left the hut.

Just as Renai had said, the thumb appeared empty. I opened up settings and there it was, a new drive I'd never seen before. I tapped it open. There were two files. I tapped on the first. The screen flickered and went black. I waited. The screen flashed again and then a file opened. I read the opening caption:

Video diary: L. Morphs,
Wom Pat district, Guam 18:06.

A woman's face came into view. She looked troubled and when she spoke she sounded nervous. I guessed this must be Lorraine, the marine biologist.

"They breathe oxygen through a sophisticated gill system located at ocular periphery when away from their marine environment. The room has to be darkened because of their photosensitivity. One of them appears ill. We are currently running tests when it is sedated. When you are near them you feel lightheaded and…sexually excited." She looked slightly humiliated by this revelation but attempted to maintain a strict scientific composure.

"On my first visit to the pool I was shown into a darkened room, not fully lights out, but dark enough to see silhouettes. That was enough. There are two caudated males, which we believe to be juveniles, because their genitalia seem to still be forming. I saw no testes, so I guess they had not yet dropped. The third, a female, was in a seclusion room. She was sick when bought in, but, ill or not, she is still powerfully built. I have been allowed to study her condition and was relieved she had been sedated. She has ichthyosis—her epidermis peels in strips. These three Aquatics have skin containing subsurface chromatophores, which can rapidly adapt with shifting colour to match their surroundings. The juvenile female exudes substantial amounts of tetrodotoxin from her cranial spine fins. That's a nerve-paralysing toxin, usually found in the Australian blue ringed octopus and in some species of puffer fish. But of course, with such a large marine dweller, the amount is greatly increased."

Here Lorraine paused and looked as if she was thinking about how to continue. She shuffled some notes out of shot.

"Examining the sedated ones is unnerving," she faltered slightly. "But it is when I am in the pool with them that things become frightening.

"The military personnel have ordered that the creatures not be anaesthetised while in water. It takes men with horrid cattle prods and chains to bind the two juveniles. These men are hardened to atrocities. I guess they have seen many awful things on remote battlefields. They bind them with leather straps so they can't attack.

"Taking their temperature and vital signs while with them in the brine pool both scares and excites me. The way they stare when you are close is frightening. Their eyes are almond shaped and the pupils large and black. It is…disturbing…to have unwanted feelings playing with your psyche."

The video went black. I waited and clicked onto the second file. The title read:

File: Aquatic Morph,
Wom Pat district, Guam 9:07

Lorraine came back onscreen. She looked a little different, tired and harried.

"Having worked closely with the sedated female I am now more familiar with her. This familiarity does not help reduce my terror in her presence. Being in the semi dark with these creatures is an awful experience. These are large Aquatics, more than two metres tall, or long, and they alter shape. I don't know how big an adult might be. They sometimes eat by pushing a sac from their mouths, much as a starfish does by extruding its stomach; other times they manage to devour their food in other ways. I'll explain that later. I don't know how many of these creatures the military have down in the lower levels. When I get out of the pool my adrenaline is pumping and I find my legs shaking. Some of my colleagues have vomited. All the men, the soldiers get erections when they are near the female. Having been in the pool with these things four times, I am now not allowed back. It's such a relief. I think the military have now found what they want from these creatures. I believe it has something to do with biological weaponry, perhaps...with the large amounts of tetrodotoxin... These creatures produce enough to equal hundreds of reef dwellers such as the blue-rings. Also, there is interest in aggregate pheromones from the male specimens' sophisticated endocrine system. It would appear the military here consider anything to be a potential weapon. For the past few days I have been kept in my quarters. They look after me quite well. They are wondering what to do with me.

"This place is huge. It sits under an old, ground-level, single-storey office block. I have seen them drive jeeps and big golf carts with covered backs along the corridors. There is a place here in this facility, called Nightmare Hall. Have I mentioned that? I think it is several levels below my quarters."

The video ended. I heard Renai's voice across the lagoon. I realised I had been holding my breath.

I looked back at the list of files and saw there was one more to be seen—I'd missed that the first time I checked. I was not entirely sure I wanted to continue. I sat for a while and remembered what Lorraine had said. Then, without thinking about what I might see, I opened it.

The screen was fairly dark, but I saw what looked to be light reflecting off glass. A caption showed at the bottom of the screen:

Aquatic Morphs,
Brine Pool, Level 3, W. Base 30:09

A camera zoomed on to show a large swimming pool surrounded by darkened glass. I leaned towards the screen on my pad and stared at two creatures standing waist deep in the water. They wore manacles about their midriffs held by chains attached to the tiles on the bottom. As I watched, trying to make out what I was looking at, one of the upright creatures lowered its bulk down into the pool and flattened itself against the water's surface. I felt there was something wrong with the shape; the thing appeared to restructuring its skeleton. It changed colour—blue and yellow flashed like neon across the mass. White and emerald green flashed back the other way. The other creature, heavily muscled, lowered itself and opened a kind of maw around the area of a rudimentary torso. This second creature flashed purple and yellow. To my horror, in the first creature, another mouthpart opened next to the first. It lifted some kind of appendage from out of the water. I saw it had elongated a section of itself and it now had hold of some kind of meat. Again the colours flashed across the thing's flattened shape. I realised what I was looking at were subsurface flesh chromatophores, changing colour, similar to a cuttlefish displaying emotion.

Although the lighting was poor I got the sense these things were intelligent. I saw the one with food deliver that hunk of flesh into one of its mouths. I couldn't see clearly, but it looked like the mouth stretched out and jerked against the meat, like a hungry calf lunging at its mother's teat. The colours changed again on the creature and, feeling a little sick at the sight, I wondered if it signified contentment.

The camera zoomed in, to see a little more detail. It was as if one of the creatures—the one not eating—knew it was being filmed. It inflated part of the flattened area that was floating upon the water's surface, then it gathered itself up and it stood. I could see a little way into the water below its waist; the water rippling so that I could see there were no arms, just elongating pseudopodia extending to the bottom of the tank. The thing now had a wide slash of a mouth above water. When it opened that slit I saw rows of shark-like teeth. A flash of scarlet spots showed all across its scaled head. The thing knew it was being watched, and it knew it had something to do with the machine above the pool. It stared at the camera and appeared to be mouthing words.

Renai was standing outside of the hut, looking in at me. He came in and sat on one of the car seats opposite. I shut the pad down, pulled the thumb drive out, and handed it back to him. He waited a moment. I suppose he wanted to give me time to think.

"That paper by the Norwegian you have. It's not much of a leap," he said. "I mean, talk of these creatures and all the books written by different people…if they aren't real, what's on the video file? What was on the *Sumatra Queen* with me? And when Marina's ROV hit the side of an undersea mountain, why did it ring as if it was hollow?"

Renai stood and walked a little down the sand and looked out over the water. I had turned the car seat around to face out to the lagoon, and from my position I could see the bulk of Mwaia. As I peered at the green swathe across its peaks and valleys, I wondered, what if? I stood and walked out of the other side of the thatch shelter and stared down onto the white sand at the edge of the water.

I wondered about the ringing, hollow sound on that undersea mountain. I had seen first-hand, growths and sea life living below the surface of the sea on the posts of harbour piers. After six months, all outward traces of the wooden pile were completely covered. I wondered how long it would take for a silt build-up to thickly cover an artificially made undersea structure. How long would be needed for a long bank to split and break away in a submarine landslide, enough to damage an undersea fibre optic cable?

Across the lagoon men were moving lumps of coral they had prised up from the sandy bottom. Renai was now over there with them again. I had not noticed him leave.

Mwaia. I thought about the fierceness and selfishness of The Kwaio Bush People, and I wondered if there really could be a hidden race, a species living alongside us. I wondered if governments were only now rediscovering this race. I heard a loud grunt from one of the men across the lagoon. Someone had cut themselves on the coral. There was blood in the water.

A while later Renai came back with two men. He introduced them as the ones who would be taking me out on board their craft for my research. This is what I had come to the Solomon Islands for, yet it was only with some effort that I was able to put aside the unsettling things I'd heard and seen since arriving. I knew I had to get on with what I had come to the islands to do. Even so, throughout the ensuing days, thoughts of what I had seen and heard were never more than pushed to the back of my mind. There was one realisation that refused to be suppressed. It was that which, to this day, even though I am now home in Auckland, still nags at me. I wonder now, if this race of beings has been living, hidden and evolving alongside humans, at what stage is their development at? I think I know the answer now. It relates directly to what I viewed in that final scene of Lorraine's video. The creature, which had been delivering the strip of meat into its chest hole, so shark like, had eaten it and had sealed the orifice before my gaze. It had raised its head and had looked directly at the lens of the camera. It now had a fishlike mouth. I watched the creature move that mouth to form words. Before the screen went black, it gave a grimacing smile, and in its terrifying stare I saw malign intent.

I have been giving much thought lately to certain tactics used by covert operators, placing themselves in the heart of their enemy's base for the purpose of gaining intelligence. I have a suspicion that the US military has been engaged in a covert war—possibly since the 40s, the end of World War II—with a dangerous and intelligent race that is indigenous to this planet.

A new war is coming. Any day now.

THE WARD OF TINDALOS

DEBBIE AND MATT COWENS

Twenty years old and I'm living in my car. I haven't slept in days. At night I park at the beach and listen to the curling whispers of the ocean. I need a shower but I can't risk it. I can't go inside.

The Hound is waiting.

The books on the passenger seat hold no comfort, no solace. They whisper of horrors unseen and lives ripped apart. Stacey's diary, heavy in my lap, screams of them.

I close my eyes and I'm fourteen again. I haven't heard of the Hound yet. Stacey is still alive. We've taken a train into Wellington unaccompanied, a thrilling taste of adult freedom. Some of the fifth formers said that there's a new cinema in town where they don't ID you if you look old enough, and *Bloodstalker's Return* has just opened. I'm tall for my age, and Stacey is what my mother refers to as a 'well-developed girl' so we figure we have a shot. Armed with eyeliner, a heavy layer of foundation and my three-inch-heeled boots, I am undaunted by the prospect. We check our reflections in the railway station mirror. Seventeen? Probably. Sixteen? Definitely.

God, we are young. The me that's watching this all play out again—watching through the gulf of time—wants to warn Stacey, just go home, just turn back and go home.

My fourteen-year-old confidence drains when we approach the Rialto theatre. It has not been a long walk from the station but the boots have pinched my toes and Stacey, spurred on by the prospect of a gory horror flick, bolts down Featherston

Street at breakneck speed, despite—or perhaps because of—my objections.

"Who would you rather be killed by: Freddy Kruger, Michael Myers or Seth Bloodstalk?" Stacey asks with a giggle as we enter the lobby and join the queue.

"Definitely not Freddy Kruger. He's the creepiest. Besides, nightmares are bad enough without actually dying in one."

"But it'd be over quickly. Blade to the guts and you're gone. Way better than being all strung up for hours while you're literally drained of all your blood."

"Yeah, I guess." An electric shudder dances up my spine as images of the first *Bloodstalker* film flood my mind.

"Seth Bloodstalk is hot, though," she adds. "If he was after something other than my blood, then definitely yes, please."

"Ew, he's like a psycho serial killer. Besides, he's dead."

"So? People can still have sex with a dead person. It's called necrophilia," she informs me.

I open my eyes, now, here in the car. A sound has brought me back, a scratching and hissing sound that chills me. I look from the roof to the glove box to the sharp lines of the armrest cubbyhole, angular behind the welcoming circles of the cup holders. A growling rumbles up from under the car.

Clutching Stacey's diary, its rounded corners smooth in my hand, I open the door and step out into the night. The ocean murmurs beyond the dunes in the darkness. I step away from the car, towards the gentle undulation of sand.

The beach disappears in a flash and I'm back in the lobby of the cinema. The scent of popcorn anchors me. Stacey is alive again. She grabs my arm as we head to buy tickets. "Hey, do you want to go halves in Jaffas?"

I nod mutely but I'm nervous that we'll be ID-ed at the ticket stand. Stacey is fearless. She smiles brashly at the young guy behind the counter and buys our tickets and Jaffas without a hitch.

We're the first ones in the cinema and Stacey darts toward the best seats, centre of the fifth row from the back. For two minutes we thrill at the prospect of being alone in the theatre, but soon a handful of people trickle in alone or in pairs. An older guy in a vinyl jacket with long greasy hair and round glasses sits right in front of us, mechanically munching popcorn. I worry that the noise will be distracting, but it only affects the first killing scene, when Seth Bloodstalker silently approaches his victim with a popcorn-crunch soundtrack that was not the director's intent.

The rest of the film is unspoiled by intrusions from the real world. If anything it's scarier, and even gorier, than the first movie. We scream aloud several times and Stacey literally jumps off her seat. We leave the cinema giddy, laughing.

"Let's go up to Courtney Place and get something to eat. I'm starving," Stacey declares. I agree and we make our away across the streets to the alleyway that leads to the city's main vein of cafes, restaurants and takeaway shops. The sound of traffic drops away as we enter the alleyway. A car park building alongside slab-like apartments form the alley's multi-storeyed walls, and they block out all surrounding noise. The hollow clacking of our footsteps echoes and our voices fall away. The concrete looks cracked and worn. The corners of the buildings are dented inwards; their sharp edges have crumbled. Empty windows glare down with the hollow-eyed stare of skulls. The bleakness of an overcast day is thicker here. We're in a dark, dangerous city street that screams it's the wrong time, wrong place. On a weekday, there would be more people, workers and shoppers. At night, there might be lights on in the buildings, drivers pulling in and out of the car park, other people walking to and fro on their night out. But on this Saturday afternoon, it feels desolate and empty.

Something grabs my shoulders from behind and I scream. Stacey erupts in giggles and releases her grip.

"Not funny," I grumble.

"No, it was hilarious. You practically jumped out of your skin," she smirks. "Did you think it was the Bloodstalker?"

"No, you just surprised me."

"Well, you should have been paying more attention. Your mind's always drifting off somewhere random."

The buildings dissolve in an instant and I'm back on the beach, damp sand pressing on the soles of my feet and crawling up into the spaces between my toes. I look up at the black expanse littered with unfeeling stars. Don't take me back, I plead to the empty night, but there's no point. I always spiral back to the beginning.

I squeeze my eyes shut and hear my words echo across the years.

"I wasn't drifting off, I was observing our surroundings, actually." My voice is defiant but I can hear the uncertainty underneath. The lost moments, the slips of consciousness I didn't understand back then.

Stacey's eyes dance around the alley walls. "Yeah, some of the murals here are pretty cool."

I had barely noticed how the scattered graffiti progresses into intricate and impressive works of art in the alleyway. Vibrant waves of turquoise and violet surround a three-eyed octopus with lurid green tentacles; a coffee-skinned angel beckons in front of a pillar, a red Samoan sei flower worn in her hair.

"I came here with Aaron after his gig in the Street Festival," Stacey says. Aaron's her cousin. He's nineteen, achingly hot and plays guitar in a band. Stacey has a huge crush on him and he's pretty cool about letting us hang out sometimes when his band is jamming.

Stacey didn't invite me to come with her to see them perform last year, though I've heard about it many times since. Some less glamorous details have fallen through the cracks in her boasting—Stacey and her brother Gareth had accompanied the band, and she'd had to lug microphones and amps up Cuba Street. No mention of the alleyway or the street art has featured in any of Stacey's previous renditions. She grabs my arm and pulls me round the corner into a narrower vein off the central alley.

From my place on the sand, in the future, I want to think that I resisted, that I suggested we turn back, go home, but I don't know what lies ahead. I don't know that I should be afraid.

On both sides the concrete walls bear giant murals. The one on the right shows rows of bullet-shaped fish with white clock-faces for heads, flying over waves against a blood-red sky. The other fills the entirety of the bottom storey of the car-park building.

It's faded and less striking than the other, less vivid and surreal. Its painted background of a night sky looming over a dead end alleyway is chipped; the murky violets and greys are scarred with scratches of exposed concrete as though cuts have been made into the wall with rhythmic repetition. Swirls of pallid mist are painted rising from the ground, creating the illusion that the thick vapour exists as much in the real world as in the mural. At the heart of the mural is a swelling darkness, which tears its way through the mist into the back corner of the alley, like shadowy claws ripping gashes through the mist. Two pale green eyes stare out from the swollen blackness, and beneath them the glint of piercing fangs, but I can see nothing else of the terrible creature. I wonder if the artist had painted it as some sort of illusion, like a magic eye trick, and if I just stare into the blackness hard enough, my eyes will adjust and the image will leap off the wall.

"It's called *The Hound,*" a husky voice informs us. I blink hard as my eyes struggle to focus on a man who steps away from the wall and turns to face us. He steps right out of the heart of the darkness and I know that he was not there before, not when we entered the alley and not when I lived this experience. Yet here he is in my memory. His wispy hair is greying and pulled uneasily back in a ponytail. His face looks as faded as his worn jeans and bush shirt but his green eyes gleam with a brightness that is at odds with his unshaven appearance. There is something not quite right about his eyes. They unsettle me.

"Yeah, tell me something I don't already know," Stacey says sarcastically. She does not seem to have noticed that he was not there a moment ago. Perhaps for her he was always there. "And I know it's cursed."

"Cursed? That doesn't cover the half of it," he replies. "That's the Hound of Tindalos. If you knew a fragment of the truth, you wouldn't look into it, lest the Hound look back."

Stacey cocks her head and stalks past him, her gaze fixed on the green eyes in the centre of the mural. She reaches the wall and turns, sticking one hip out. "So it's fine for you, but not for us? Do you think the Hound sees me now?" She rubs her hip against the mural and smirks.

He yanks the sleeve of his shirt up and examines the three wristwatches strapped to a heavily tattooed forearm. "Almost," he says breathlessly. "Time will tell."

"They haven't even painted a hound. It's just eyes and teeth in a black mess," I mutter, rolling my eyes.

Fourteen-year-old me is beginning to feel uncomfortable but boredom is an easy mask for my fear. There is something too intense about the old guy, and worse is the way Stacey looks at him. I have seen her flirting with boys at school and the hot barista at the corner cafe, but the three-watched man gives me the creeps.

Stacey walks up to him; her curiosity makes her brazen. "Tell me," she insists, her voice lower. "I'm not afraid."

Behind the wall, beyond the paint, a scratching begins. The three-watched man smiles and whispers to Stacey. He presses something round into her hand. I can hear the raspy panting of a beast, rushing down the alleyway like the fury of a gusting wind. My muscles clench at the lick of cold air against my neck. Then I find I am standing alone on a darkened beach once more. Stacey and the three-watched man lay far across the ocean of years. I inhale the fresh salt air as sadness fills me once more. The waves whisper a lullaby. I am so very tired.

My eyes close, and when they open the mural stares back at me. Stacey crosses to it in two quick strides, her eyes wide.

"Hey, I see it now! I can see the Hound." Stacey lifts her arm, gesturing at shapes in the dark void of the mural. "Those are its front legs and that, in the corner… is its head?" Her voice wavers slightly.

I look again and see nothing in the black paint. I wonder if Stacey's faking it but when she turns to me her face is such a strange mix of awe and pale unease, I know she really believes.

"Step back," the three-watched man warns suddenly.

To my surprise, Stacey obeys without comment and hurries to me. She clutches my arm, squeezing too hard. Colour creeps back to her face but her eyes are like flashlights and her breathing is heavy and agitated.

"It's in the corner," she whispers.

"What corner?"

"Where the pillar sticks out of the wall." She points at the edge of the blackness and I see the wall is not flat as I'd thought. There are square columns protruding every couple of metres. The mural has been painted to create the illusion of a flat surface but once you see the columns, it is clear the black space is sunken in between the pillars.

"The corner. Do you see it?" Stacey asks. She hasn't released her grip on my arm. It's starting to hurt. I go to pull her hand off but the sight of her whitened knuckles looks pathetic somehow; her hand seems small and childlike, and I change my mind.

I lift my gaze back to the painting when a low rumble growls through the alleyway. The ground shudders. The coiled barbed wire atop the alley's side fence rattles, and the old concrete bones of the building groan.

The three-watched man smiles and pushes his sleeves back down. He points back the way we came and shouts, "Run!"

Years of school drills and advice to "Stop, drop and hold" vanish as the tremors increase and we sprint out of the alleyway. The tremors kick up dust in a cloud behind us and I lose sight of the three-watched man.

The ground shifts and I find myself back on the darkened beach, my feet sunken into sand, my breathing hard and fast. I let the fresh chill in the air, the soothing hiss of rushing waves lull me back to the present and the illusion of safety. Pale moonlight washes over my bare arms. My burns have healed faster than I hoped. Spindly black lines emerge from the edge of the scabbing wound on my forearm like spider's legs. There's barely a trace of ink left under the scab. I've burned it clean.

I'm back in Wellington. The earthquake is over but my legs still feel shaky and uncertain. We're nearly at the station. I can see the building looming overhead.

I have to tell her. The compulsion to share, to check I didn't imagine it, is overwhelming.

Stacey barely lifts her face from her phone as words tumble out of me about how the mist on the painting had shifted when the earthquake started, how the shadows had crawled out of the walls.

She doesn't look at me but replies, "I know. I saw it. It was the Hound."

On the train ride home Stacey is glued to her phone. She tells me she's found a video, The Truth of Tindalos on YouTube. I turn down her offer of one of her ear plugs, fear gnawing at my stomach at the sight of the unblinking man ranting wildly from the screen. Whether it's the creepy guy or the earthquake or the unspoken fear that something terrible is clawing its way into the real world, I just want to forget.

I stare at the other passengers, try to imagine their names or jobs. My reflection in the train window looks back at me with sad, old eyes. I'm only a kid and a voice inside me whispers that it is the beginning of the end.

Stacey is still watching the video when we arrive at our station. There's something in her hand, a metal disc. It's hard to see past the phone but it looks like a brooch or medallion. The pattern reminds me of the tattoos on the three-watched man's arms. When we part ways it seems as though there is something cruel in her distractedness, her indifference.

The world doesn't end right way. Our friendship drifts. She changes and I pull away. When I make the effort to hang out, she speaks of nothing but some strange new website she's discovered, or bizarre theories about dimensions. I laugh it off and try to put it all in the past, but I can sense the invisible threads stretching back to the alley, pulling her down the path she's on.

Then Paul from my Geography class asks me out and it proves to be the final nail in the coffin of my close friendship with Stacey. His best friend's girlfriend, Hannah, is fun, relaxed and so much cooler than me. Hanging out with her is easy and, for a while, if I don't see Stacey, I can forget.

In a flash of laughter and a long-held breath released, it's the end of school. Stacey isn't around for graduation. Her dad died in a car crash when she was sixteen. I spoke more with Stacey's mum than her at the funeral. Her mum has always liked me. Stacey and her mum have moved away now, and have faded from my thoughts like the girls I met at summer camp when I was ten. She never posts on her Facebook account or replies to the group messages she used to be part of. She has become a ghost, virtually and physically unseen. Yet I think of her as we file out of the auditorium on the last day, finally free of school. I think of her when I see a young man with close-cropped hair, green eyes and a wispy beard standing in the bus shelter, shifting from foot to foot. He looks familiar. It's not until I'm in bed that night that I remember Stacey and take a moment to wonder where she is. It's not until then that I realise the bulky bracelets the man was wearing were probably watches; three watches.

Moments later I'm on the beach, I'm twenty, I'm living in my car and terrified of dying. I want to bury myself in the cool sand, to hide forever. I cannot hide from the past. I fall back into it again and again. The ward, which I'd hoped would hide me from the Hound, has cursed me. My sense of time has unravelled as I sink further into the vortex of swirling memories and fears and relive them all.

Stacey dies during the summer of my first year at university. I've just turned nineteen. A friend from high school shares a story from a local paper in Hamilton on social media. The death, though horrific, has not yet made it into the national news cycle.

The body of a young woman has been found in a dead end alley late at night, her corpse savagely dismembered, only identifiable through dental records. The photo of Stacey accompanying the article belies the brutality of the event. It is a recent picture, the article says. She's older, her cheeks narrower, her jaw line more pronounced. Her hair has grown longer and darker, and in the photo she has it in a braid that coils back over her shoulder. She wears a black tank top and has tattoos of black, spiralling runes scrawled down her shoulder and arm. She's looking at the camera, alive and relaxed. Her eyes accuse me; hazel-green, intense, and lonely. She looks like she knows death is coming for her.

I travel up to the funeral with four old friends in an aging Toyota Corolla with a boot barely big enough for all our bags. The sight of five stuffed overnight bags and backpacks buried under a layer of neatly pressed black suits and dresses still wrapped in drycleaner's plastic seems as incongruous as the trip itself. We laughingly swap memories and stories of Stacey and, more generally, of high school, as though we are mourning both. Somewhere along the Desert Road the mood shifts. Tina suggests we listen to some of Stacey's music. She's downloaded one of Stacey's old Spotify playlists. The first track is *When September Ends* and, listening to that, I weep hard, ugly tears.

Harsh sunlight strikes through the right side windows as the road bends and I'm ripped out of the car.

I find myself sitting in a strange, small room. Sketches of runes and hideous monsters fill the walls around me. My left arm is splayed and upturned on the vinyl armrest as I recline in a chair, staring numbly at the black lines being etched into my skin with the buzzing needle. I glance at the man wielding the tattoo gun. Long string-like hair sticks to his neck with perspiration, jet-black, unlike the grey stubble on his face. His black vest clings tight to a round belly but exposes his wiry arms, which are heavily tattooed with a maze of runes, writhing tentacles and peculiar creatures with preternaturally large eyes and gaping mouths. I cannot make sense of how the shapes fit together and yet it fills me with cold fear when my eyes fall upon his arm.

I turn away and see her journal on the table beside me. It is open to a page with the heading 'The Ward of Tindalos' and the sight of the intricate design fixes me in the chair. It's a spiralling coil of many clock-faces bearing unrecognisable numerals, wrapping over one another like a ball of string. I feel the needle clawing my skin like a cat scratching a door as the tattoo grows slowly across my arm.

On the beach I run my fingers over the scab where I have burned the tattoo out. Weeks earlier I take the knife blade off the camp-burner flame and press it into my arm. My screams echo through time.

My eyes open as the sound of the engine dies and I see Tina's Corolla has pulled to a stop. My friends tell me I have slept for most of the drive. Stacey's funeral is held in an old brick church just north of Hamilton in Rototuna. We walk through a steepled door, sit in pews, and mumble our way through the hymn neatly printed on the crisp service leaflet. It is reassuringly like every other funeral I've been to apart from the strange mix of guilt and dread that flows in and out of me like a tide. This isn't for some old aunt or uncle or even a grandparent. It is for Stacey, Stacey who is a month younger than me. Her face smiles beatifically on the paper leaflet as though defying the idea of death.

I catch sight of Stacey's mum glancing at me as we leave the church and again at the graveside. I fear she blames me for drifting away from Stacey, that she wonders why I stand there living while the remains of her daughter are lowered into the ground.

She speaks to me at the reception and there's nothing but warmth in her voice. "So glad you could come." Her lip trembles and she clasps my hand with cold fingers. "Come back to the house, after this. There's something of Stacey's I want you to have."

The house is small but neat. Stacey's room is down a short hallway, the door open. "You go ahead, dear. I just need the loo," her mum says.

At first the room is not empty. There's a girl sitting in the wood-backed chair by the mirror, leaning forward and staring at her reflection. She doesn't move as I step into the room. Stacey didn't have a sister—not one that she knew about. I can't see her face but this girl looks so much like Stacey, the way she looked when we were friends.

The toilet flushes and I look over my shoulder. When I turn back the girl is gone. I stumble a little; sit heavily on the edge of the bed. The room lurches under my feet and a scratching sound starts up. It's behind the walls, in the corner.

"Stacey wanted you to have this, I think."

Stacey's mum is holding something out to me. She's smiling a sad, thin smile. In her hand is a notebook, a journal with rounded edges. She presses it into my hands and pats my shoulder. My fingers close around the journal and the scratching intensifies. My ears are ringing.

"I don't think it made her happy, but it kept her busy."

I look down at the book, at Stacey's handwriting on the cover, and I realise that I'm crying. I'm crying out of fear. The walls feel close, too close. I push myself up to my feet and barge past Stacey's mum. The scratching follows me down the hallway to the front door, but once I'm out of the house, back under grey clouds in the open air, the noise fades. I clutch the book, mumble my condolences, and flee.

I stumble forward, nearly falling into the hard sand. I glance up at the stars and breathe the smell of the ocean, the darkness embracing me as I lift my leaden foot and take another step.

I'm back in the small and musty room of my student flat. The lamp by my bed throws little light and in the dimness the walls seem to shrink and draw close. I read Stacey's journal with an exhausted, desperate hunger. It only partly makes sense. She was terrified but excited about the possibilities of time and other dimensions. One of the first pages describes a visitor, a tattooed woman with her dark hair pulled back in a long braid who came to Stacey's bedroom at night, who spoke from the shadows with a warning not to look any deeper into the Hound or the three-watched man. A warning that only inflamed her curiosity. There are printed out pages stuffed into the back of the journal, photocopies of old books and photos of manuscripts. I close my eyes and the journal sits behind my lids, floating in my mind's eye in a pool of light on a reading desk I have never owned, never seen.

I open my eyes and all the time in the world has passed. I've dropped out of University, drifted away from friends. I'm scared to be indoors. The corners of rooms fill me with dread. I hear the scratching of the Hound everywhere. I feel the nearness of its raspy breath when I close my eyes. I have found the sketch of the Ward of Tindalos in Stacey's journal. I hope that may keep me safe.

I blink and the gnawing tattoo gun etches my skin. I open my eyes and the painting in the alley fills my vision with shifting blackness and hungry green eyes.

I return to the beach. The enveloping darkness of the present wraps around me but I feel no comfort. All is lost. The ward could not save me from the Hound even as I spiral through the tightening coils of time.

I thought I had escaped. I thought I had slipped through the web that caught Stacey. I'm standing in the alley, the same alley with the mural in front of me, the journal in my hand and the tattoo fresh and pink-rimmed and pulsing on my arm. I know that the more I fight the tighter the web will close around me. But what can I do but fight?

I shift the journal to my left hand, step closer to the wall and form a fist with my right hand. The murky blackness of the mural stares back at me. I slam my fist into the wall, the impact sending a shockwave up my forearm. The pain comes quickly but feels distant, impossibly far away. I punch the wall again, and again. Small circles of darker black begin to form where my split knuckles leave blood spots on the wall. I hit it again. Tears are hot behind my eyes, ready to fall, but I blink them back and strike the wall again. I draw my fist back and open my mouth to scream but something grabs my wrist. I spin around, my voice swallowed, and meet the gaze of the three-watched man.

His beard is long and grey, his hair thin and his face deeply wrinkled, but it is he.

"What?" I croak.

"It's time," he replies. "She threw it off the scent for a moment, but I'm tired of running."

He lets go of my wrist, gently pushes me aside. He's muttering something in a language I don't recognise. I back away, closer to the mouth of the alley. The air shudders and I hear the scratching, the terrible scratching that haunts my dreams. Darkness is gathering in the corner of the alley. I want to turn, to run, but all I can do is stumble backwards, my eyes fixed on the shape of the old man as mist spills out around his legs and the darkness grows in front of him. There is a shape there now, a deeper darkness which moves on long limbs, prowls forward. The three-watched man drops his arms and falls silent as the air splits and the ground begins to shake. I see a thick, barbed trunk snake forward and grip the front of his body. Terrible dark limbs reach out and begin to pull the man apart as his torso contorts and collapses, his insides sucked out and into that gnawing darkness that I cannot look away from.

I hear my own voice screaming, screaming as I run through dust and panic. I am fourteen, running from the alley. I am twenty. Stacey is beside me, is dead, is visiting herself in the past to warn of this day. I'm half blind with dust and tears but ahead of me I see two girls of fourteen running from the darkness of the alley into the light. I stumble, fall, drag myself up onto bloodied knees, onto clumsy feet, into streets unfamiliar and uncaring. I run until my lungs ache and red mist creeps into my vision. The girls are gone. The three-watched man is gone. For a time, I am gone too.

I try to burn the ward off, to fix myself, to undo the damage. The pain rips me back to the cinema, the alley, her funeral; her journal.

The more I struggle, the tighter the web becomes.

And then I'm here, on the beach. Darkness and sand and the soft lapping of the waves comfort me. I recall a fragment from one of the books Stacey found, a translation of a passage about R'lyeh. A sunken city, a dreaming city. I look back at the lights of Wellington and for a moment I can hear that terrible scratching again. I feel the dark eyes of the Hound searching for me.

Perhaps I can find sanctuary. Perhaps I can be safe? Down in R'lyeh, where Cthulhu lies dreaming, maybe my own dreams will be quiet. There will be nothing but waves, and sand, and the soft curves of a world beyond the Hound's reach. I stand, drinking in my last taste of the wind, of the night air. It's time to go where the Hound cannot follow. I walk out into the water, Stacey's journal clutched to my chest, and I step beneath the waves.

A BRIGHTER FUTURE

GRANT STONE

Samuel had been quiet the whole trip, but when Peter pulled the van into the driveway he gave a squeal of delight, jumped out and ran to the door. Then ran back and rapped on the windscreen. "It's locked."

"Course it's locked," Peter said. "There should be a key under a pot plant out the back."

Samuel ran off again.

"Looks nice enough," Lisa said.

Peter looked at the house. "It's new at least."

"You don't like it?"

"It's fine."

"Better than fine, little brother. It's a year's worth of free accommodation in the most expensive part of Auckland.

"Well, there is that."

Lisa opened the back of the van. "You going to sit there all day, or do I need to set up your new, already-furnished, free house all by myself?"

Peter walked through the front door to the smell of fresh paint.

Samuel shouted from upstairs. "I call dibs on the corner bedroom!"

It didn't take long to unpack, but by the time they'd got things sorted they were all exhausted. Peter went out for fish and chips and they ate them at the kitchen bench straight from the paper. Peter had worried that Samuel might be too nervous to sleep.

But by the time dinner was finished he was already yawning and his eyes closed as soon as his head hit the pillow.

"Dad?"

Peter hesitated, his hand over the light switch.

"You're really good at looking after me. I'm glad you're my dad."

"I'm glad I'm your dad too, buddy. You're my favourite child."

"I'm your only child."

Peter kissed Samuel on the forehead. "Still counts. Now sleep. You've got a big day tomorrow."

Lisa had made them both a cup of tea. "Have you seen this?" She handed Peter an envelope. Inside was a small card: 'On behalf of all faculty and students, please allow me to congratulate Samuel Wilson on winning the Blake scholarship and welcome you both to the Saint Enoch family. Welcome to a year that will change your life.'

"Well, that's nice, isn't it?" Lisa said.

"Yeah," Peter said. "It's just that after the last couple, I'd was quite looking forward to a boring, non-life-changing year."

Lisa put the cups on the coffee table. "Oh, honey. Come here."

I'm not crying, Peter told himself.

Lisa held him until the worst had passed. His tea was cold by the time he sat down and took a sip. He didn't mind. "I keep telling myself I'm over it," he said, "that I can move on. But it keeps hitting me when I least expect it."

"It's not either-or, little brother. You'll never be over it," Lisa smiled, "but you have to keep moving, for Samuel's sake. Coming up here is the right thing to do—a year at one of the best schools in the country. There's been, what, three Prime Ministers who attended Saint Enoch's?"

Peter snorted. "That's not necessarily a ringing endorsement."

"Come on. You're setting him up for anything he wants to do in the future, and it's what Melanie wanted. She applied for the scholarship, didn't she?"

"Yeah," Peter said. Melanie hadn't said anything to him about the scholarship as far as he could remember, but it was possible she'd mentioned it. She would have applied at the start of February and by the end of that month things were changing so fast Peter could hardly think. He had found the acceptance letter in a pile of bills on the coffee table in June, and by then he couldn't ask her. She was still breathing then, but only technically. The machines were doing all the work.

Peter blinked. Lisa had been saying something. "What?"

"Hurry up with your tea. It's not just Samuel that's got a big day tomorrow."

He tipped the remains into the sink. "Sure you won't take the bed? I don't know how much sleep you're going to get on the couch."

"I'm not kicking you out of your bed on your first night in the house. Anyway, the couch might be great and the bed terrible."

"Thanks for helping us get set up."

"We're family, little brother. It's what we do."

The sound of heavy shoes stomping down the stairs made Peter look up.

Lisa was already in the hallway. Samuel stood on the bottom step wearing his new uniform. The blazer was too big and his trousers flowed over his just-polished shoes like a robe.

"Christ, Peter," Lisa whispered. "He looks like a rich wanker."

Lisa wrapped Samuel in a hug that he grudgingly permitted. "You look so grown up."

"I look like a rich wanker," Samuel said.

"Samuel Aaron Wilson," Lisa said, "what kind of language is that? Be careful—I hear boys who talk like that get their mouths washed out with soap at Saint Enoch's."

Samuel looked frightened.

"Hey," Peter said. "Buddy. They don't do that. Aunt Lisa is pulling your leg."

"I know," Samuel said. The look on his face did not change.

"It's all boys. No girls at all."

"You told me you didn't like girls."

"When I was eight. I'm eleven now."

"So you like girls now?

"You know what I mean. It's just weird, a whole school with no girls." Samuel looked in the rear-view mirror, twisting his tie. "And I don't like this. Feels like I'm being strangled."

"You'll get used to it," Peter said. "It's good to know how to knot a tie. You'll need to wear one when you're out in the real world."

Peter had already driven past the school entrance three times, looking for a place to park. He'd seen a few gaps, but nothing big enough for the van.

"You don't wear a tie."

"I'm wearing one today."

"Today's different."

A BMW pulled out just ahead. An Audi on the other side of the road saw the gap the same time Peter did. He pulled in before the Audi could move. The van lurched to a stop. Something heavy in the back slid across the floor and crashed into the opposite wall.

It was nearly eight-thirty. The footpath on both sides of the street was a sea of blue blazers. Every other vehicle was black or silver, mostly Mercedes' or BMWs. There were no other vans. Parked next to a cluster of Land Rovers was a red Porsche convertible. A balding man leaned against the driver's side, talking on his phone, nearly in the middle of the road. Nobody seemed bothered.

"Dad, I—" Samuel blinked, looked away.

"It's okay, Samuel. I get it. You're thinking this is a giant mistake. You want to go back to Thames, your old school, your old friends, our old life. The next few weeks won't be easy, but we'll get through. Before long you'll be walking around like you own the place."

"I know. I'm just scared, I guess." Samuel wiped a palm across his eyes.

Peter blinked. "Fear of the unknown is nothing to be afraid of."

"It's not that. It's just—" He gestured at the window. "I don't mind the new school, but I don't want to change. I don't want to change into one of them."

"That's never going to happen." Peter brushed a speck of dust from the shoulder of Samuel's blazer. "Just because you wear a rich wanker's uniform doesn't make you one. You'll always be you. You'll always be my boy."

"Dad! Language!"

Peter raised his hands, "Sorry, buddy. But it's true."

Samuel sniffed. "Thanks, Dad."

The bald man was still on his phone. He seemed to be staring straight at Peter, although it was impossible to tell. He wore mirrored sunglasses, the kind that always made Peter think of American cops.

Peter unclipped his seatbelt. "Come on then. Let's get in there and see what's so special about this school where you need to wear a tie."

Principal Bridwell met them at the door of his office

"Peter Wilson," Principal Bridwell wrapped Peter's grip in a fist like a shovel blade. "And this must be Samuel. Welcome to the Saint Enoch's family."

The wall behind Bridwell's desk was covered in framed certificates.

"How have you found Auckland so far? Getting used to the traffic? Quite a change from Thames, I bet."

"It's a bit busier, yeah." Peter found his mouth suddenly dry. He left school twenty years ago, got married, built a career and raised a kid. A memory surfaced: him and Martin Morgan in Form Two, waiting outside the headmaster's office. Waiting to be asked who threw Martin's bag and broke the window.

"And you're a builder, I understand?"

"I run my own company these days. Well, I did. I'm wrapping up a couple of projects back in Thames, and then I'll be looking for something closer. Although the way the property market is at the moment, going back to swinging a hammer might not be a bad idea." Peter realised he was waffling and closed his mouth.

"Indeed. And Samuel. I'm sure you're keen to meet your new classmates."

"Yes…yes sir." Samuel stared at his shoes.

"No sirs round here," Bridwell said. "I know we don't look it, but Saint Enoch's is a modern, progressive school. Call me Alastair, if you'd like."

Yes sir—I mean Alastair." Samuel raised his eyes up like he was looking at Father Christmas. Bridwell smiled.

Someone coughed in the doorway.

"Ah. Fullerton. Come in," Bridwell said. "This is Samuel Wilson and his father. Samuel's the recipient of the Blake scholarship this year."

Fullerton inclined his head. "Welcome to St. Enoch's." There was a smile on Fullerton's face, but it felt more mocking than friendly.

"Fullerton is a prefect in your year," Bridwell said to Samuel. "He'll look after you until you've got used to things. You're in the same homeroom. Speaking of which, you should both be there," Bridwell looked at his watch. "Now," he said at the same time as the bell rang.

"Come on then," Fullerton said, already halfway to the door. Samuel gave a backwards glance but by the time Peter opened his mouth to say goodbye both boys were gone. He thought of Samuel blinking back tears in the van fifteen minutes ago.

"He'll be fine," Bridwell said. "Fullerton's a good lad. His father attended St. Enoch's. His grandfather too. Fullertons are part of the fabric of the school.

"Yeah," Peter said, sounding more confident than he felt. "He'll be fine."

Bridwell leaned back in his chair. "I'm glad you decided to take the scholarship. Fullerton isn't the only third-generation student. It's good to see past pupils return with their children. But it's nice to get some new blood too."

Peter tried to smile. "We're happy to be here."

"There's a small social event in the hall this Friday evening," Bridwell said. "I'd be honoured if you could attend."

"I'll be there," Peter said. "We both will."

The street was nearly empty by the time Peter got back to his car. A crumpled muesli bar wrapper lay on the passenger seat, the remains of Samuel's breakfast.

Peter heard the front door slam, then footsteps on the stairs. By the time Peter followed, Samuel's door was already closed. Peter leaned in but couldn't hear anything. The door opened just as he raised his hand to knock. Samuel had changed into jeans and a black sweatshirt. His uniform lay crumpled on the floor.

"So? How was it?"

"Fine."

"That's it? Just fine?"

"Just fine."

"Can I get you something to eat?"

Samuel shook his head. "I've got homework to do."

"You sure? I can—"

"Sorry, Dad." Samuel closed the door.

Lisa had a little more luck over dinner.

"It's okay," Samuel said, "Might take some getting used to."

"In what way, honey?"

Samuel pushed macaroni cheese around his plate. "I dunno. Just different."

"What are the teachers like?"

"Just teachers."

"What about the other kids," Peter asked. "How's that one who took you to class…Fullerton?"

Samuel stopped chewing. He stared at his plate for a while, then took a sip of water. "He's okay."

"Well you're a real mine of information," Lisa said.

Samuel shrugged again and smiled. "Sorry. There was this big ceremony in the afternoon but I can't tell you anything about it. They swore us all to secrecy." There was the hint of a smile on Samuel's face, so small Peter wondered if he was imagining it.

Lisa looked up from her laptop. "He's got a bruise."

"What bruise?"

"Christ, Peter, you really are blind sometimes. On his arm. Thought it was weird, him putting on that sweatshirt. I went and had a look once he fell asleep."

Peter was already out of his chair. "I'll go wake him up."

"Sit down, you egg."

"It's only his first day at the school. If someone's laid their hands on him I'll—"

"You'll do nothing. Not yet. Leave it until he's ready to talk. Otherwise he'll clam up and never say a thing."

"How do you know?"

"Because that's what you do."

Peter flipped through the channels but there was nothing on.

"I could talk to Bridwell tomorrow."

"What are you going to tell him? Your son's got a bruise you haven't seen and he won't tell you about? He's a good kid, Peter. He'll talk to you. Just give him a few days to get used to things, huh?"

"Yeah, but—" Peter found himself stifling a yawn.

"Look at you. Just as worn out as Samuel. Go get some sleep."

"But the bruise..."

"Will still be there in the morning. Worry then. Sleep now."

Peter let himself be bundled off to bed. He turned off the light and stared out at the darkness.

Peter woke feeling like he hadn't slept at all, but that couldn't be true. The dream was proof of that. He lay in the darkness, trying to grab on to whatever was left, but he could only summon a single image: a long plain of cracked earth. He was alone under a purpling sky. Though it was cold, the stars rippled as if viewed through a heat haze. The plain was absolutely barren—no trees, or even rocks—just that earth, cracked as if it hadn't seen rain for years. And although the plain was empty, Peter knew there was something just beyond the horizon. He knew what it was, he realised. Or at least, in the frustrating way of dream-logic, he remembered having known what it was. But even that thought was fading now. He felt a weight on his chest and for a second he struggled to breathe.

Then the dream and the suffocating feeling were gone.

He swung his legs over the side of the bed and took a few more deep breaths. The air felt stale in his lungs. In the last few weeks of Melanie's illness, he'd woken like this every morning: terrified, struggling to breathe as if he were drowning. But he hadn't experienced any since she died, until today. He pulled himself to his feet and went to make breakfast.

Being up early had its advantages. Someone from the school had done a pretty good job of stocking the fridge and pantry. Peter found eggs, bacon, wholemeal toast and some expensive looking coffee. By the time Samuel wandered downstairs, already dressed, but still rubbing his eyes, Peter had put together a feast.

"What's this?"

"Breakfast."

"Expecting a rugby team to drop in?"

"Aunty Lisa has to go back to Thames today. Thought we should send her off properly."

"She has to go? So soon?"

Lisa emerged from the bathroom, still towelling her hair. "Things to do and people to see, I'm afraid. But I'm not far away. I'll pop back up in a couple of weeks."

Nobody talked while they ate breakfast. Peter had hoped he'd be able to catch a glimpse of Samuel's bruise, but he couldn't see anything through Samuel's long-sleeved shirt. Samuel ate quickly and walked away from the table before Peter was halfway through his coffee.

"What's the hurry?"

"Thought I might walk to school this morning. I want to get out the door early."

"Really?" Peter put down his cup. "Aunty Lisa's bus doesn't go until eleven. There's plenty of time for me to run you to school."

Samuel shook his head. "Nah. It's okay. I just want to walk."

Peter shrugged. "Suit yourself."

"What do you think?" he asked after Samuel had headed back upstairs. "Think he's trying to keep me from asking about the bruise?"

"Maybe. But maybe not. Perhaps he really does just want to walk. Get a feel for the neighbourhood."

"Maybe."

Lisa stifled a yawn.

"You'll be pretty happy to get back to your own bed," Peter said.

"No, I was right. Your couch is actually really comfortable. But I kept waking up. Weird dreams."

"How do you mean weird?"

"You know, just weird."

"You're as informative as Samuel." Peter grabbed the empty dishes from the table and carried them to the sink.

"It was like I was lost. In some kind of desert?"

The plates slipped from Peter's grip. Most of them landed noisily in the sink, but one smashed on the floor. Peter stood, barefoot, amidst sharp shards.

"Ah, you egg. Look what you've done. Don't move." Lisa went to fetch the broom.

There was no sign of a bus when they arrived. He walked Lisa to the stop but they were the only people there. "Sure there's a bus coming?"

"We're just early. You were in too much of a hurry to get me out of the house."

"That's not—" he started to say, but Lisa held up a hand.

"I'm only yanking your chain. I know it's going to be weird. Call me any time you need, okay?"

"I'll wait with you."

"Unnecessary, little brother." She pointed to the departures sign. "Thirty minutes. I can look after myself for thirty minutes.

Anyway, looks like I'm not the only one who turned up early."

A black Saab stopped on the other side of the road and a man in a suit climbed out of the passenger side. He didn't have any luggage. He crossed the street, checked the departures sign and stood next to the bus stop.

"You're sure?"

Lisa snorted. "Dude. I'm a grown-ass woman."

"Call me when you get back to Thames?"

"It'll be the first thing I do. Now go do something important, you fancy Aucklander."

Just before he turned onto Manukau Road Peter took another look in the rear-view mirror. Lisa had her head down, looking at her phone. The man was reading a newspaper. Peter pulled out into the traffic.

He told himself he wasn't waiting near the door just so he could get a glimpse of Samuel when he got in. But it was nearly three thirty and there he was, sitting at the kitchen table where he had a good view of the living room and the front door beyond. When he heard footsteps on the path outside he put down his coffee cup.

Samuel came in quietly, almost bent over. His hair hung in front of his face.

"Hey, Buddy," Peter said, hoping the fear he felt didn't carry in his voice. "How was your day? Can I get you something to drink?"

Samuel shook his head.

"Everything okay?"

Samuel looked up. The bruise ran from his cheekbone to the corner of his eye. "I told you Dad," Samuel said, "Everything is fine."

Peter took a step back. "Who did this to you?"

Samuel didn't speak.

"You need to tell me, Samuel. I need to make sure Principal Bridwell is aware that—"

"I can handle it."

"Samuel, this isn't something *you* need to handle. I'll call Principal Bridwell now."

"You won't tell anyone," Samuel's voice was so soft it was almost a whisper. But there was a strength behind it that made Peter look at his son again. The bruise stood out stark and angry on his cheek. But Samuel's face was expressionless.

"Samuel, it's not fair, I'm your father," Peter could hear the whining in his voice and he hated himself for it. He fell silent.

Samuel stared at Peter, waiting to see if he was going to say anything more. Peter lowered his head. He felt like he'd just lost an important battle.

Samuel turned away. "I've got homework."

Samuel didn't emerge from his room for the rest of the evening. Peter sat downstairs, flicking through channels on the TV, but not settling on anything for more than a couple of minutes. Several times he found himself standing, walking halfway to the stairs, but forced himself to sit back down. He wanted more than anything to talk to Samuel, but he still felt sore from the conversation earlier, as if he were the one with the bruise, not Samuel. He paced, did the dishes, then a load of laundry.

Lisa didn't call, which didn't surprise Peter at all. She would have had every intention of letting him know she'd arrived safely for about five minutes after getting on the bus. Then she would have found some interesting gossip on her phone and forgotten completely. He picked up his phone a few times, and then put it back on the coffee table. He knew what she'd say if he told her about the new bruise. She'd tell him to get on the phone to Bridwell right away and let him know. Then she'd be up all night worrying too.

So he sat. He felt a pressure building around the sides of his skull. He closed his eyes and took a few deep breaths. After Melanie's diagnosis he'd started suffering from panic attacks and they always started like this. Then he'd get agitated and have trouble breathing. He'd tried to hide them from Melanie. After all, what was a little freak-out compared to what she was going through? But she was too smart for that. *It's okay*, she'd say, as if she hadn't been chugging painkillers all day. *Just let it out. Close your eyes. Breathe.*

So he sat and he closed his eyes and he breathed. Eventually he felt the pressure easing. He leaned back on the couch and looked up at the ceiling. His head felt clearer, as if he'd been for a walk around the block.

He went upstairs. Samuel's door was closed. He knocked and when there was no response he quietly opened the door. Samuel was already in bed. New textbooks were stacked up on his desk. It annoyed him that Samuel hadn't bothered to say goodnight. Samuel looked younger when he was asleep and Peter felt a pang of loss. How many times had they stood just like this, him and Melanie, looking down at their boy's face? Back when the future was as open and unmarked as Samuel's new exercise books.

It had to be Fullerton. Peter thought about the look the boy had given him in Bridwell's office. A rich kid with attendance at Saint Enoch's as a birthright—the little psychopath had probably tormented Samuel and didn't even think about it afterwards. He'd go in to school tomorrow. Bridwell would be shocked to hear that Samuel was being bullied, especially in his first week. He'd sort it out. It would feel good to call Lisa, let her know he'd sorted everything.

Peter closed Samuel's door.

He was walking barefoot on the plain of cracked earth. The sky was not quite the same as it had been in his last dream. The purple hue was darker now. The air had a sharp, acidic taste, something like iron. He wondered about the dust he was kicking up with every step. Perhaps it would be wise to stop walking, let the dust settle.

Something was over the horizon. Then he felt a twist, as if his mind had seen what was there, then quickly turned away, as if it was trying to protect him from something he should not see.

But he had to see.

He willed himself to move forward. A breeze picked up and

he coughed against the dust. He hadn't gone more than fifty paces before the wind became a sandstorm. He closed his eyes but he could feel the sand rasping against his skin. More than anything he wanted to stop, turn around, and run the other way. He knew with the certainly of dream logic that if he did the storm would cease, but he lowered his head and took another step, then another.

The wind screamed in his ears and stole the air from his mouth.

Bridwell was in a meeting so the receptionist asked Peter to wait. He took a seat on a couch next to a cabinet full of trophies. The walls were covered with framed pictures of past students in poses of triumph: a film director receiving an Oscar; the captain of the Auckland Blues hoisting the Ranfurly shield; a faded newspaper article from the eighties featuring a bespectacled man in a suit under the headline 'The Ten Million Dollar Man'.

Prominently placed off to one side, the award-winning photo of the current Prime Minister from last year's profile in *The Guardian*. Barefoot in the wet sand of Bethells Beach in winter, hands thrust into the pockets of his expensive jeans, smiling at something behind the photographer. Paul couldn't stand the guy, had never voted for him, but he'd read the article. It was little more than a puff piece but he could understand how his party had swept into power in a landslide two years ago. In the article the Prime Minister had spoken of his time at St. Enoch's in glowing terms. There had always been a small number of boarding students and the now-Prime Minister had been one of them when his parents were killed. They had been returning to their home in Napier after a day trip to the beach at Waimarama. The 1958 Bedford truck was unregistered, with three bald tyres. The driver was well past eighty and had not held a driver's license for two years when his left arm went numb, his chest began to burn, and the truck drifted over the centre line. 'I wouldn't be here today,' the Prime Minister had said in the profile, 'and I certainly would not have become Prime Minister without the drive and persistence I was taught in five glorious years at St. Enoch's.'

That sentence had probably resulted in a 20% increase in fees the next year.

Peter noticed his leg was jiggling up and down. He stopped it and took a few deep breaths. He heard Melanie's voice in his head again. Just let it out. Close your eyes. Breathe.

"Mr. Wilson?"

Peter opened his eyes.

"You can go in now," The receptionist said.

Bridwell came out from behind his desk. "Mr. Wilson, so good to see you again. Please, take a seat." There were a couple of chairs and a low table in the corner of the office. "Would you like a coffee?"

Peter shook his head. "No, I'm fine."

"How is Samuel adjusting to life at St. Enoch's?"

"He's…well, there's a problem. He's—" Peter had been running this discussion over in his mind all morning, but here he was and he couldn't get the words out. "He's…I think he's being bullied."

Bridwell's looked dismayed. "Oh my, and this is still only his first week."

"Well, yes. It's—"

"What makes you think he's being bullied?"

"He comes home and goes straight to his room. I've barely seen him the last couple of days."

Bridwell nodded. "The first few days at a new school can be tough, particularly when you're adapting to a new city as well. He's probably overwhelmed with everything. Perhaps he's just exhausted when he gets home."

"He's got a black eye."

Bridwell didn't say anything for several seconds. "Oh dear," he said. "You must be feeling terrible."

"It doesn't matter how I feel. Someone is hitting my son!" Peter could feel his face flushing red. He hadn't meant to raise his voice.

"As I'm sure you know, we take a zero-tolerance approach to bullying at St. Enoch's. If someone has been bullying your son, you have my word I will find out."

"Wait—what do you mean *if*?"

"You say he has a black eye, but we don't know what happened. I'll talk to his teachers and some of the prefects and try to get to the bottom of what happened." Bridwell smiled, obviously an attempt to calm the father down, but the sight of it just made Peter angry.

"But he's being bullied! It's that prefect that took him to class yesterday."

Bridwell frowned. "That's a serious accusation to make Mr. Wilson. What makes you think Fullerton might be harming your son?"

Peter started to reply. Closed his mouth.

Bridwell smiled softly. "I'll find out what's been happening and let you know. I'll be in touch. Don't worry, Mr. Wilson. I've been a Principal for many years. I've found that these things have a way of working themselves out. "

He was obviously being dismissed. Peter wanted to say something, to let Bridwell know what he really thought of his precious St. Enoch's, but instead he found himself on his feet, walking towards the door.

"Oh, Mr. Wilson."

Peter turned.

"I do hope we'll see you at the mixer this Friday night. It's a chance for you to see a different side to the school. I think you might really appreciate it."

Peter found himself smiling, hated himself for it. "I'll see you there."

The house felt like a prison when he returned home. He'd already made the beds and tidied the place before his meeting with Bridwell, so there was nothing to do. It was going to be a scorcher of a day. He should make the most of being an Aucklander now; do some exploring, visit the shops, go to the beach, but he was shattered. Those bloody dreams had ruined his sleep for the whole week. They hung around during the day too. Several times he'd closed his eyes just for a couple of seconds and found himself back there, walking barefoot on that cracked plain under those glistening stars. He blinked. Had he nodded off standing in the kitchen? For a second he thought about taking himself back to bed, but he had never slept well during the day, and he didn't think today was going to be any different. He put a couple of spoons of instant coffee in a cup. Then he added a couple more.

He called Lisa again while he waited for the kettle, but there was still no answer. He left her another message. His voice echoed in the empty kitchen.

He looked up at the ceiling. Samuel's room was directly above the kitchen.

He stood in the doorway, holding an empty plastic bag. *I'm not spying*, he told himself. *I'm tidying*.

Samuel's room was spotless. He'd made his bed, just as he'd done the last two days. The first couple of times Peter had been impressed—Samuel had never been so tidy at home, but something about the perfectly turned-down duvet, completely free of wrinkles, felt wrong.

He crouched down and peered under the bed. Normally he'd expect to see half-finished muesli bars and potato chip wrappers, along with several week's-worth of laundry, but it was spotless.

Peter opened the top drawer of the dresser. Socks on the left, underwear on the right, perfectly organised. The next drawer was full of t-shirts, perfectly folded. Samuel was just a kid. Kids were supposed to be messy and smelly and complain about cleaning their room. They didn't turn into neat freaks overnight. It just didn't happen.

There was something balled up at the very back of the bottom drawer. Peter had to stare at it for several seconds before he could understand what he was seeing—one of Samuel's new white uniform shirts. Whatever had happened to the thing, Samuel couldn't have been wearing it at the time. One of the arms had been ripped off completely. The arm that was still attached was shredded with long, straight cuts that ran from shoulder to cuff. And on the front was a bloodstain larger than his fist.

He dropped the shirt. It lay on the floor in the middle of the bedroom like something dragged from the sea. After a while he picked it up again and shoved it back in the bottom drawer where he'd found it.

The afternoon passed with nothing to show for it. He wanted, needed, to talk to Samuel about the shirt, but he couldn't see how. If he mentioned it, Samuel would know Peter had been in his room, but it wasn't as if he could say nothing. He couldn't stop thinking about it. Peter had always been a confident parent, from the moment he'd first heard Samuel's newborn cry. At every phase in their life together he'd somehow known exactly what to do, what to say. Even at the worst of times, the last few weeks of Melanie's life and the desolate months that followed, his relationship with Samuel had always been there. They still had each other, and he'd thought they always would. He suddenly felt like he was living with a stranger.

Samuel didn't arrive home until nearly five. Peter jumped up from the table when he heard the door rattle and nearly ran across the kitchen. He forced himself to slow down a little, then stopped dead when he saw.

"What happened?"

Samuel's sleeves were rolled up. He raised his right hand. His knuckles were raw. Samuel clenched his fist and fresh blood began to flow. It ran down his forearm to his elbow and dripped on the floor. Samuel looked at his own blood as if it were an exotic insect he was seeing for the first time.

"I told you not to go to Bridwell. I told you I could handle it."

A slow smile spread across Samuel's face, turned into a sneer. "It's been handled."

A buzzing started in Peter's head. He took a step backwards, felt his back hit the wall.

"I need a shower," Samuel said. "And then I have homework." He looked down at the blood fallen from his fist, a stain now spreading across the carpet. "Clean that up."

Peter closed his eyes for a moment. When he looked again Samuel was gone. Samuel didn't leave his room for the rest of the night and when Peter woke the next morning he found himself alone.

He'd been telling himself a story the whole afternoon. Samuel would come home and say he didn't want to go. They'd go out to dinner instead, check out a movie. They'd gorge themselves on ice cream and popcorn, stay up too late and sleep in the next day. It would be the perfect evening, just the two of them. But Samuel came home and went straight to his room, without a word.

Peter waited as long as he could. Then he went upstairs and knocked on Samuel's door. "Hey, buddy? You still keen on going to this thing tonight? We could skive off and go see a movie instead. You know…if you wanted?"

Samuel opened the door, but only a crack. "No. We're going."

"Oh. Okay. Well, I was just wondering-"

The door closed again.

Peter's suit was still hanging on the back of the door, right where he'd left it. He'd taken it off as soon as he got back from dropping Samuel off at the school on Monday. Wearing a suit twice in a week. The last time he'd worn it was Melanie's funeral.

He tried to call Lisa a couple more times. When her recorded voice asked him to leave a message he hung up. He'd already left enough.

Samuel appeared in the living room just before seven. He was wearing his uniform, tie straight, shoes polished.

"Looking sharp son," Peter said. Samuel shrugged.

Samuel didn't say a word the whole drive. Peter kept wanting to say something, anything, to break the silence, but he kept quiet as well. There had been a Saint Enoch's monastery once, back before the school. Peter didn't know if the monks were the kind that took a vow of silence. Perhaps that had something to do with the way all the conversations he tried to start with people from Saint Enoch's sputtered and died. Even with his own son.

He gripped the steering wheel and looked out into the night.

Peter hadn't been in the school hall before. Even if he had, he might not have recognised it. Thick red curtains hung from the ceiling, hiding all the gym equipment. Jazz played through the PA speakers. If it were not for the lines of the basketball court still visible on the floor, Peter could have sworn he was at a yacht club.

It was crowded. All the men wore expensive suits. The women wore thin, silky dresses. Peter pulled at the collar of his shirt again. His suit hung awkwardly on him, as if he'd recently gained weight, or lost it.

Bridwell was waiting near the door. "Mr. Wilson. So glad you could make it. Good evening, Samuel."

"Good evening, Alastair," Samuel said, and the familiarity in Samuel's voice was like a dagger in Peter's back.

Someone called from across the room. A group of kids were leaning against the wall. Samuel walked over to join them.

"Could I offer you a drink?"

"Thank you, yes." *God, yes.*

A table near the door was covered with plates of canapés and bottles of wine. Bridwell poured two glasses, handed one to Peter and raised his own in a toast. "To new beginnings."

The wine was really very good, and strong. Peter's head began to spin after a couple of sips.

Fullerton pulled himself away from the wall and wrapped his arms around Samuel's shoulders. Peter expected Samuel to flinch, but he leaned in to the hug and pounded Fullerton on the back as if they'd been best friends for years.

Fullerton said something and all the boys, including Samuel, burst out laughing. Peter wondered if he'd been wrong about the older boy. And if he'd been wrong about Fullerton, perhaps he'd been wrong about everything. The image of Samuel's torn and bloodied shirt rose again in his mind, but it suddenly seemed far away and unimportant.

Peter raised his glass again. "To St. Enoch's."

The wine was really very good.

Bridwell walked him around the room and made introductions. Peter smiled but wasn't capable of much more. It might have been the hum of conversation, but Peter struggled to make out the names and professions Bridwell rattled off. This one was a newscaster. That one had just retired from a twenty-year political career. There were lawyers, doctors, and members of the boards of the largest companies on the New Zealand Stock Exchange. Bridwell just kept moving him from one handshake to another. The smiles didn't reach their eyes. There was an excess of teeth. And suddenly Peter's head felt far too heavy. He took a step back, stumbled, fell against the wall.

"Are you okay?"

Peter blinked. Bridwell was leaning over him, a concerned expression on his face.

"I'm... Yeah. Fine. Just tired. Good wine." He looked at his glass and was surprised to see it was already empty.

Bridwell nodded. "I haven't given you the grand tour yet, have I?"

Peter shook his head.

"Come on then," Bridwell said. "A walk might clear your head a little."

He looked back as they left the gym. Samuel was still laughing with his friends.

The cold air hit him as soon as they were out the door.

Bridwell set out towards the playing fields at a brisk pace. Peter walked faster, struggling to keep up. When he reached the middle of the field Bridwell stopped. "Beautiful, aren't they? There's so much light pollution in Auckland, but out here you can still see a few. I'm sure you're used to a far less polluted sky out in the country."

Peter looked up. There was a halo of light from houses on the other side of the fields, but if he looked straight up he could see a few stars: the Southern Cross, Orion's belt.

"It's funny" Peter said. "I never really thought to look up."

Bridwell nodded. "We get so tied up in the minutiae of life. I'm the same. Whenever I'm working late I come out here before I head home. To remind me what's really important."

"The stars?"

Bridwell smiled. "What about you, Mister Wilson? What's the most important thing in your life?"

Peter didn't have to think about it. "Samuel. There's nothing else now. I'd do anything for him." Peter was surprised to hear the words tumble out of him, even though they were true. The fog might have faded from his head, but he was obviously still feeling the effects of the wine.

"I understand. I feel the same way about the students."

The school chapel was on the other side of the playing fields. "The chapel is older than the school," Bridwell said. "In fact, it's even older than the monastery that was here before the school. It was built in 1865. Back then it would have been the only stone building for miles. The stars must have been spectacular."

Bridwell produced a key from his pocket and placed it in an ancient lock. The door opened with a creak. "Sorry," he said. "I keep meaning to ask one of the caretakers to oil that. A five-minute job, but I never seem to remember. Something more important always crops up."

They stepped through the door into darkness.

Bridwell flicked on a torch. Peter couldn't see much of the interior, just the backs of wooden pews and the shadow of an altar at the front. Bridwell waved the torch towards the wall. Hidden in a small alcove were steps leading down. "Be careful here," Bridwell said. "Bit of a Health and Safety nightmare, I'm afraid."

Bridwell started down and Peter followed. He couldn't see anything apart from Bridwell's back and the tiniest of lights from the torch. The air grew colder. There was a damp smell that reminded him of iron.

"Ah. Here we are."

Peter felt the last stair. He stepped down onto rough, uneven rock. They seemed to be in a cave.

Bridwell turned off the torch.

"Good one," Peter said. "Could you turn the light on again before I trip and break my neck?"

He couldn't hear Bridwell at all. He waited, concentrating on the dark, but the only sound was his own breathing.

"Fine," Peter said. "If you're going to be a dick, I'll see you outside." He turned around, stretching out his foot for the step, but he stumbled against the wall.

He had to be close to the stairs. He reached into his pocket for his phone. The screen was so bright it nearly blinded him. He winced and waved the phone across the wall, but it only showed what some deep part of him already knew. There was no staircase.

He followed the line of the wall, looking for an explanation. His fingers found the answer before the light did: a metal door, flush with the surrounding rock. So Bridwell had lead him down here, then silently backed away and closed the door. "Missed your calling," Peter muttered. "You should have been a comedian."

He refused to panic. He wasn't going to give Bridwell the satisfaction of a freak out. "You private school people are all the same," he muttered. "Just a bunch of wankers."

He took a few steps away from the wall. It was a big space. The light from his phone screen didn't reach the ceiling.

He was surprised to find his phone still had a signal. There weren't many numbers on it. He selected Lisa and hit dial. His phone beeped and connected. Something buzzed on the other side of the room and Peter saw a light. Bridwell pulled a phone from his pocket, stared at the screen for a moment, then hit a button. Peter's phone disconnected.

"You would have been proud of her," Bridwell said. "She put up a good fight. She screamed when Luther dragged her to the car. If there had been anyone else around, or if the bus hadn't been late, she might have made things complicated for us."

"Where is she?" Peter couldn't hide the tremor in his voice.

Bridwell dropped Lisa's phone on the floor. The screen went black as it crunched under his heel. "It doesn't matter," he said.

A hand grabbed Peter's wrist and his phone slipped from his grip. The screen flashed once as it clattered across the floor, and in that instant he saw the others surrounding him.

"You can scream too, if you want." The voice in his ear was barely a whisper, but Peter recognised it. Fullerton. He struggled uselessly. The boy was stronger than he looked.

"The chosen see visions sometimes," Bridwell said. "Tell me, Mister Wilson, have you experienced any strange dreams lately?"

There was light now, just a little. Two students stepped towards him, each holding a small candle. They looked like altar boys, except they weren't in white vestments. They wore heavy robes, deep red, except where age had faded them to a pallid grey.

"I know we seem like—what did you call us? A bunch of wankers, but we're proud of our ways. They burn in us, just as they did in our Founder."

"What the hell are you talking about? Saint Enoch was the mother of Saint Kentigern, the daughter of a Scottish king."

"I didn't know you were a student of religion."

"I Googled it."

"Ah. Well. It's a common misapprehension. Our school is named for Enoch Bowen, the greatest of all saints, though not a Catholic one. A great man, and an endless source of wisdom. He gives us so much and asks for so little in return."

He heard shuffling. Something brushed against the back of his legs. People were on their hands and knees behind him. Fullerton and another boy pushed him gently backwards until he was lying across the backs of children.

"Don't feel too bad, Mister Wilson. It's not your fault. What with your wife's unfortunate situation, no close friends, no family except a sister who won't be missed, there was nothing you could do. You were a sparrow in a hurricane from the moment we delivered the letter."

Another robed figure emerged from the darkness.

It was Samuel.

"You don't need to worry. I will look after your son," Bridwell said. "I've never seen a child adapt so quickly. There's no telling what he'll accomplish when he leaves school armed with everything he'll learn from us. From *them*."

Something moved just beyond the circle of light. At first Peter thought it was Bridwell, but the shape was too tall and thin, a shadow without a man to cast it, darker than its surroundings.

He turned his head and even in the absence of light he could see several more shadows. They loomed over the children like expectant parents.

Samuel held a long dagger with a curved blade. Peter searched Samuel's face and found no trace of the boy he'd been a week ago. He thought again of the shirt he'd found in Samuel's room. It had been Samuel's shirt. Had it been Lisa's blood?

Samuel climbed on top of Peter, the boy's knees digging into Peter's chest. He struggled to breathe.

Samuel raised the dagger above his head.

When the blade caught the candlelight, it shone like a star.

THE SHADOW OVER TAREHU COVE

TRACIE MCBRIDE

Renee's stomach turned as her wife Marika threw their little hatchback into the turns on the narrow country road. They were halfway to Marika's family marae to attend a tangi, and it had just occurred to Renee that she'd never attended a funeral. Of course, she had known grief and loss, from losing childhood pets to a handful of heartbreaks from failed relationships prior to meeting Marika, but her friends had always enjoyed robust good health and fortune, and, incredibly, there had been no deaths in her family since she was a baby. Accompanying Marika to farewell her grandmother, not only did she have to contend with the unfamiliar protocol of a three day tangi in the company of mostly strangers, but in supporting her wife in her grief, she would be navigating treacherous waters. Not one for extravagant displays of emotion at the best of times, Marika tended to retreat inside herself when enduring great stress or turmoil, like a wounded animal hiding in a cave, and it was Renee's job to venture in after her and coax her back out—preferably without getting bitten in the process. If she were to be honest with herself, Marika's guardedness was partly what drew Renee to her; she had been both challenged by her reserve and rewarded when she became one of the elite few to break through it.

Renee glanced at her wife in profile, Marika's expression inscrutable, and her queasiness intensified. For better or for worse, that's what she had signed up for, hadn't she? She looked back to the road and braced herself for another blind corner.

Renee barely knew Marika's grandmother, and found the tangi emotionally exhausting. She could only imagine how hard it was for Marika. She'd been uncomfortable at the thought of sleeping in the same room as a dead body, but that apprehension was put to rest with more practical concerns of sharing her sleeping space with dozens of snoring, farting strangers. She slept lightly, waking often, while the songs and speeches carried on through the night.

Occasionally during the day she wandered into the kitchen, picked up a tea towel or a potato peeler and made vague efforts to help out, but mostly she made an effort to stay away from the others. Marika's family wasn't openly hostile or deliberately rude, but they had a way of flowing around and away from her, making space for her only temporarily, and grudgingly, as if she were a foreign body cast into the stream of their busy lives.

The morning of the interment dawned misty and unseasonably cool. Renee prepared herself as best she could in the shower block, peering into the mirror above the hand basins to apply makeup. They changed shoes for the walk up the paddock to the cemetery. Marika took Renee's hand, the first prolonged touch they'd shared in a couple of days, and they took up a position near the head of the funeral procession. By the time they reached the graveside, Renee's palm was sweaty in Marika's grip.

Somebody began to keen, a mournful sound that made Renee uncomfortable. Marika rested her head on Renee's shoulder and relaxed enough to share her bottled emotions. She sobbed, her tears soaking into Renee's suit jacket. The bush-shrouded hills, the swirling mist, the moist air carrying a hint of salt from the coast, so alien from the diesel and dust and concrete of the city she was used to, threatened to drown her. As the wailing intensified with more women taking up the call, and the priest intoned his final words, Renee swayed on her feet. Marika's arm tensed to keep her upright, and for a moment it was Marika having to prop her up, not the other way around.

With the formalities over, there was still some business to which

Marika needed to attend. Renee managed to persuade her to book into a motel rather than prevail on the further hospitality of family. There was only one choice within a fifty-kilometre radius, a little sixteen-room affair adjacent to the local pub. Both establishments looked like they were stuck in a 1970s time warp. While Marika did her thing—she could not be persuaded to let Renee tag along—Renee read, napped, grazed on stale packaged snacks from the service station nearby, and made a desultory attempt at exercise by assuming a few yoga poses, before abandoning the endeavour for want of a yoga mat. The prospect of a pub dinner that night had never seemed more enticing.

Carrying her third mixed drink back from the bar, Renee approached the table and found Marika talking with another woman. Renee saw the newcomer brush a fingertip across the back of her wife's hand. Renee was drunk and in no mood to behave civilly. Rather than risk making an arse of herself, she retreated to a corner of the bar to nurse her pride.

A thin old woman nearby was staring at her. Renee was surprised when the woman spoke.

"You studied at Miskatonic University." It was a statement, not a question, delivered in a slurred yet surprisingly authoritative voice.

Renee blinked, wondering how this stranger would know that. The old woman held out her hand and Renee felt obliged to hold it.

"They call me Kitty, Aunty Kitty to my face, Crazy Kitty behind my back." Her grin spread further, her eyes sinking into folds of skin, her body shaking with soundless laughter. "I was visited by bigwigs from Miskatonic once, ya know. When I was a kid. Want to know why?" Her demeanour shifted, no longer jovial. She leaned close to Renee and fixed her with an almost desperate stare. Renee smelled alcohol, unwashed flesh, and a hint of cow shit.

"Umm…" Renee leaned away and cast her gaze over to Marika, hoping that she might come to her rescue, but Marika was still talking to the other woman, oblivious to Renee's absence. Kitty waved a near-empty glass under Renee's nose, and she was grateful for the comparatively wholesome scent of yeast and hops.

"Buy me a drink, and I'll tell ya."

Her wife's companion whispered in Marika's ear, eliciting a laugh and a playful shoulder bump. It looked like nobody was going to save her from Crazy Kitty any time soon. With a resigned nod, Renee took the proffered vessel and headed for the bar.

Renee had found the term: "non-US ethnic minorities only" somewhat patronizing for a Kiwi teenager with limited life experience and modest family means. Nevertheless, she convinced herself that a scholarship to an overseas university was too great an opportunity to disregard. She had been delighted to learn her application was successful, and she spent the months between acceptance and arrival in Arkham fantasizing about how amazing her stay was going to be.

Even before she'd arrived at Arkham she made a new friend, a young Indigenous Australian woman named Jida whom she met at the bus terminal, and who was attending Miskatonic on the same scholarship. Alongside this new companion, her arrival in the university town built beside the Miskatonic River, with its Gothic architecture, was just as she'd pictured it, but that was about where fantasy and reality parted ways. They'd barely stepped off the bus when they were set upon by rich white boys (that being the dominant demographic of the student body) to join this club or that, most of which were esoteric in nature. One tall, earnest young man with an abnormally high forehead strode up to Jida.

"Are you the Māori girl taking marine biology?" He pronounced it 'may-OR-rye', and Renee suppressed a wince; no doubt he wouldn't be the only one to mangle the word. Jida pointed over her shoulder at Renee.

"You've got to join the cryptozoology club," he said to Renee, looming over her. "You simply must." Then, to Jida. "You too, I suppose, maybe, if you want."

"Why not?" Jida had said with a shrug and a smile. "It could be good for a laugh."

At first the two brown-skinned women from the Antipodes were the subjects of intense scrutiny. The other members grilled them on various aspects of their culture, in particular their knowledge of the creatures of their myths and legends. Jida strung them along for months, spinning fanciful tales that bore little resemblance to real Dreamtime stories, and weaving in hints of extra-terrestrial encounters and alien abductions that seemed to greatly excite the group. Renee lacked the imagination to play the same game, all her answers being variations on: "That's just a story—it's not meant to be taken literally," and, "I don't know anything about that." If the truth be known, she found the earnestness of the other members, and their deep longing to believe, a childish and unnerving trait in young adults who were meant to be aspiring scientists and scholars. Yet she lingered in the club long after the others lost interest in her, for reasons she was never fully able to articulate.

Outside of the club, the local students viewed them with a certain degree of resentment, their scholarships being perceived as an undeserved 'free ride'. Rather than her horizons broadening, Renee found her world shrinking. She seldom ventured further than the lecture hall, library, and the dilapidated accommodation wing in which the administration corralled all the foreign scholarship students.

Jida transferred back to an Australian university at the end of the first year.

"Sorry, darl, this place gives me the shits," she'd said as she kissed a tearful Renee goodbye.

Following that, Renee felt adrift. She managed to stick it out and complete her degree, but it was more out of a lack of anything better to do than a true drive for achievement. Upon returning to her home soil, she all but wept in relief, and soon put conscious thought of the oppressive atmosphere of Miskatonic Uni out of her mind. She must have taken in more than she thought during her time in the crypto club, though. Any chance she got, and even for some opportunities she manufactured, she would talk at length about yetis and Bigfoot and other such creatures, until she gained a reputation as being 'a bit of an odd fish'. Eventually she learned to keep that strand of specialised knowledge to herself.

Now here she was, over a decade later, in a fusty old country pub at the arse end of the world, catapulted back to her memories of those early days at Miskatonic by a chance meeting with the local nut job.

"...they wanted to know about the *Ponaturi*."

"Huh, what?" Renee was barely listening to Kitty. Marika must have finally noticed Renee's absence and looked around the bar for her; both she and her friend were staring at Renee. Marika scowled and gave an exaggerated head shake, a pantomimed warning: don't stand too close to the crazy lady, it might be catching. In a drunken act of defiance, Renee lifted her chin and pointedly turned away.

"The *Ponaturi*. I saw them take my cousin from the beach. Took her to their underwater caves, and we never saw her again. They might have taken me, too, 'cept I was only little, and I ran and hid under a log. I can still remember it—me tucked in tight in the dirt, and those ugly fuckers snuffling and shuffling through the bush trying to sniff me out..." For a moment Kitty looked lost in her recollections, her rheumy gaze distant and her half-empty glass threatening to slip from suddenly slack fingers. Then she shuddered and brought herself back to the present. "It happened at Tarehu Cove. You ask your girly over there about it." Kitty nodded towards Marika. "Only land access to that beach is over her family farm. 'Course, she'll probably tell you it's bullshit, but she knows." She gestured to encompass the patrons of the bar. "They all know," she muttered in a tone laced with bitterness. She drained her glass in one swallow, thrust it into Renee's hand and smacked her lips together wetly. The sound made Renee queasy. Everything was making her queasy—the press of poorly washed bodies, Marika's distance, the excess of booze she'd consumed, Kitty's incomprehensible tale—and she had to hold onto the bar, close her eyes and take several deep breaths before she was able to order another beer for Kitty. Marika had spoken fondly and often of the secluded little cove she had frequented in her youth, but Ponaturi? She had no idea what that was about…

Except you've heard that word before, haven't you, Renee? In a dusty room in a far off land, mispronounced by American accents. You've heard the word, listened to the stories, imagined the stench and the slimy touch of their amphibian limbs, dreamt of the creature's loathsome faces, and woken up screaming…

Renee elbowed her way back through the crowd and held the beer out to Kitty. At the same time, someone took hold of her other arm in an ungentle grip. Renee yelped, startled, and nearly spilled the beer. It was Marika, looking grim. The woman she'd been talking to was nowhere to be seen.

"It's late. I'm tired. Let's go," Marika said. She glared at Kitty and began to steer Renee away.

"Wait!" The old woman clutched at Renee. For a moment she was caught in a tug-of-war. Just before Marika could wrench her free, Kitty leaned in and whispered in Renee's ear:

"If you go down to Tarehu Cove, make sure you don't stay past dark."

Lying skin to skin in bed with Marika, alone at last after what felt like weeks, Renee should have been feeling amorous, but couldn't summon up the energy. Still, her hand crept across Marika's chest to idly toy with her nipple. Marika exhaled softly and shifted to press a little more closely against her.

"That old woman in the bar, Kitty…" Renee began. "She tells me you know something about the Ponaturi."

Marika's mood turned icy in an instant. She grabbed Renee's wrist and pulled her hand away from its ministrations. "Don't," she commanded.

"Don't what?"

"Don't start with that crypto shit. We're here so I can spend time with my whanau, not so you can indulge in your weird little hobby."

Renee forced a laugh. "Oh, no, of course not. I only mentioned it because...well, she's a bit loony, that Kitty, isn't she? Lucky you came to get me when you did, otherwise I might never have gotten away from her."

A pause, then a non-committal, "Hmmm." Marika's face was unreadable in the dark, but she must have accepted the excuse; she relaxed back against the mattress and released Renee's wrist, then turned on her side with her back to Renee. Renee contented herself with draping her arm over Marika's waist.

"Hey, I've got an idea," she murmured against Marika's neck. "We're not in a big hurry to head home tomorrow, are we? Why don't you show me that cove you've told me about? The one that the tourists can't find? It sounds really romantic..."

"Yeah...Yeah, okay, I'd like that."

Minutes later, Marika was asleep, a state that was much later coming for Renee. She should have been looking forward to a seaside tryst with her soul mate—so now that it was confirmed, why did the prospect of visiting Tarehu Cove infuse her with dread?

They slept late the next day, and when they woke, Marika was in a much better mood, toying with Renee's feet under the table at brunch and flirting with the shop assistant at the general store to secure a small discount off the two gaudy beach towels they purchased. The drive to the beach took them off tarsealed roads and onto several winding kilometres of gravel that challenged their urban vehicle's suspension, then onto a long, dirt track that led ultimately to a padlocked farm gate bearing a hand-painted "Private Property—Keep Out" sign. The sign writer had used too-thin red paint and the letters had run slightly, making the warning appear fresh and bloody. Marika pulled on the hand brake and got out, winking at Renee through the windscreen as she approached the gate; not at the padlocked end where logic dictated it would open with a key, but at the opposite end. She hefted the gate off its hinges and swung it open.

"We all got sick of trying to keep track of the keys, so Aroha came up with that idea," she explained when she got back into the car.

"Aroha?"

Marika dismissed the query with a wave. "She's a cousin…"

Who isn't around here? Renee thought sourly. As if on cue, a figure appeared on a small hill in the distance. As it grew closer, it resolved into a young woman riding a bay mare at a gallop. Just when it looked like they might vault the bonnet, the woman reined the horse in sharply. Renee recognised her as the woman talking to Marika in the bar the night before.

Marika's introductions were made more awkward with Aroha looking imperiously down on them from astride her mount. The woman was dressed in a faded T-shirt dotted with holes, black shorts and grubby gumboots. She rode bareback, her muscular thighs gripping the horse's sides, her long and untamed black hair stirring, Medusa-like, in the breeze. If it weren't for her tatty attire, she might have resembled a warrior princess bent on striking down a rival.

"We're heading down to the beach," Marika told Aroha. "Renee wanted to see it." She looked sideways at Renee, smiled and took her hand. At this display of affection, Aroha stiffened, sending her horse skittering slightly. Renee smiled smugly back.

"Didn't happen to bring your dive gear, did ya?" Aroha asked.

Marika shook her head.

"I've got *one* spare set," that emphasis on 'one', green eyes flicking towards Renee and away. "Come out on the boat if you want. It'll be just like old times." Another pointed glance at Renee, meaning: *there is no place for you here.*

"Thanks, but nah. We're just after a bit of alone time." Marika squeezed Renee's hand.

"Yeah, well…" Aroha jerked her head in the direction from which she came, indicating a long, single-level dwelling positioned for panoramic sea views. "You know where to find me if you change your mind."

The track to the beach traversed a couple of kilometres of gorse-studded paddock before disappearing into dense bushland. The final stretch had to be travelled on foot. Laden with towels and picnic supplies, they picked their way carefully through the undergrowth for several hundred metres, following a creek on a gentle downward slope.

They emerged abruptly from the bush onto sand. Renee stumbled and righted herself, almost breathless as she caught the first sight of the glittering and boundless stretch of sea. The beach was tiny and pristine, a horseshoe-shaped sliver of paradise, delicate wavelets lapping the shore. A pohutukawa tree in full bloom jutted from a small cliff, providing just enough shade for two. Beyond that cliff, Marika had told her, lay another much larger beach, easily accessible at low tide and also frequented by Marika and her cousins. But Renee had little interest in exploring the other side, not when this spot seemed crafted just for them.

Marika was already stripping off, leaving her clothes in a trail to the ocean's edge as she whooped and squealed in a childlike rush to dive beneath the water. She came up gasping and laughing, clutching her arms across her bare chest in a futile gesture of self-protection.

"What's it like?" Renee called.

"Fucking freezing!" Marika called back, before throwing herself backwards into the brine again.

Renee was more cautious to get in—most of her underwater activities were undertaken in a five millimetre wetsuit, and she was too well schooled in the dangers of hypothermia to take the chill lightly—but soon the sun, the solitude and Marika's infectious delight had her acclimatised and splashing with glee alongside her lover.

Sometime later hunger called. They ate as they had bathed, completely naked, towelling off only enough to keep salt water from dripping onto their food, and letting the air dry them completely. When Marika finished eating, she smoothed out her towel and reclined on it with a sigh, arching her back to press her breasts and belly skyward, then fell back into stillness with her eyes closed.

Renee took a moment to drink the sight in—small conical breasts, smooth brown skin stretched over lean muscle and classically sculpted cheekbones, large, bony hands and feet that earned her much teasing from friends and family but only drew Renee's admiration, for their implications of strength and capability. *And mine, all mine...* Renee's gaze wandered up from those hands, and thoughts of what Marika could do with them, to her mouth, lips slightly parted in a contented smile, made Renee smile too.

"You've got a crumb on you," Renee said. "Right—here." She leaned over and kissed the corner of Marika's mouth. She began to draw away, and Marika caught her. With a giggle, Marika rolled, pulling Renee over until their positions were reversed and Marika had Renee pinned beneath her. Marika kissed her back, open-mouthed and desperate, almost violent in her desire, and it was Renee's turn to arch up, offering herself to Marika's heat.

Renee woke to a moment of disorientation. Her mouth was dry, and everything ached—had they been drinking? Then her memory kicked in. They'd made love on the beach, and it had been urgent, vigorous, transcendent. Then they must have fallen asleep. Now it was dark, she was cold, sand was stuck and scratching in delicate places, and she needed to pee.

Marika had managed to cocoon herself in both beach towels. She breathed heavily, not quite snoring. A sudden, sharp surge of tenderness speared Renee, and she left her wife to sleep on. Moonlight showed their scattered belongings only as vague, shadowy lumps. Renee felt about the beach until she found shoes and a T-shirt, and made her way bare-assed up the beach to find an appropriate spot in the bush to urinate. It was strange, she mused as she squatted and released control on her bladder, how deep one's conditioning went; she knew they were alone and there was next to no chance they'd be disturbed, and she'd been only too happy to have sex in the open air, but the minute she had to take a leak, here she was taking the trouble to hide behind a tree.

Two things intruded on her senses at once—a soft splashing sound, at first indistinguishable from the splatter of urine on the ground, and a faint but repugnant odour of rotting fish. Both came from the direction of the beach, and Renee peered around the tree trunk in search of the cause.

Someone…no, some*thing* stood on the beach. It was a humanoid shape, but only superficially; its head was too narrow, its eyes too bulging, its posture too distorted, and its hands and feet were webbed, unlike any human Renee had ever seen. Its belly gleamed palely in the moonlight, the rest of its scaly flesh a darker hue, and its back bore a stubby dorsal ridge.

The creature turned and gave a croaking bark, and on its signal, several more narrow heads arose from the water. Renee counted five, seven, eleven…they kept on coming, emerging from the sea until some two dozen of the things stood on the sand. Their fishy stench flooded the air, and Renee choked back a retch. A burst of adrenaline zinged through her body, urging fight or flight. Or freeze.

Renee stood rigidly still, pressed against the tree trunk as if she sought to sink into it, and all but held her breath. The creatures hopped and shambled and loped up the beach, their misshapen feet slapping obscenely on the sand; heading straight for Marika.

They swarmed to surround her, and stood looking down on her for a few moments. Then two of them bent to grab her and haul her to her feet. Renee cried out, suddenly heedless of her own survival, but she was drowned out by the screams of Marika herself, who was suddenly wide-awake and struggling. The towels fell, revealing her nakedness, and the creatures bayed and hooted with what might have been appreciation, or lust.

Another two took hold of Marika's legs, and they lifted her off her feet. She bucked and writhed against their grip. Several more shuffled forward to take hold of her at various points along her limbs. Renee imagined their putrid, clammy touch, and retched anew. Now Marika was virtually immobilised and held aloft, facing the moon like an offering. They carried her in this fashion into the sea until they stood waist deep in the water, with a whimpering Marika floating on her back in their midst. Two of the monsters at the head of the procession took deep, chest-inflating breaths. One of them bent to press a lipless mouth to Marika's. She fought it, but it wrapped a hank of her hair in one webbed claw to hold her in place.

When Renee realised what they intended, it broke the spell on her fear-frozen limbs; she sprinted from her hiding place towards the sea; too late. They dived with eerie synchronicity, taking Marika under with them. When Renee reached the water's edge, not even bubbles remained to mark their passing.

She was lucky not to break a limb in her frantic, stumbling passage through the bush and back to the car, and lucky not to completely lose her mind as she scrabbled through the bundle of belongings she'd swept up from the beach in the search for the keys. After far too long, her fingers closed on cool metal. She set the car on the straightest line for Aroha's house on the hill, heedless of dips or bumps or gorse, the wild ride jolting her dangerously in her seat until she connected with a rudimentary driveway that provided a smoother path.

She was still pounding on Aroha's front door when it opened. Aroha appeared annoyed at the disturbance at first, but at the sight of Renee, her eyes widened and she took a step back.

"What the—?"

Renee looked down at herself and realised the cause of her shock; in her rush, she'd paused only to put on underpants, and blood streaked her bare legs from several scratches and scrapes she'd sustained running through the bush. She shook her head.

"It's Marika. They took Marika! We have to go get her back."

"Just, just slow down, calm down. Who took Marika?"

"I don't know, the...the frog fish men things. The Ponaturi!"

Aroha stared at Renee in silence.

"I'm not crazy!" Renee blurted. "I know what I saw!"

More silence. Then, quietly, sadly, as she began to turn away—"I can't help you."

"Wait!" Renee grabbed Aroha's arm and played her trump card. "You love her, don't you?"

A range of emotions played over Aroha's face. After a lengthy pause, she sighed.

"Alright. Come in. But you have to understand—it'll be dangerous, and a long shot. No guarantees we'll be able to save her, and we'll have to wait until tomorrow night. They only come to shore after dark, so that's when we're most likely to find her unguarded."

"Okay, okay, whatever you say," Renee said, nodding furiously. She started to follow Aroha inside, then stopped. "But how do you even know where to start looking? They took her into the ocean, for fuck's sake! She could be fucking anywhere!" Her plan to charge after Marika and her captors, all guns blazing into the sea to mount a rescue was looking more and more nebulous by the minute.

Aroha barked a short, mirthless laugh. "Oh, that's the easy part. We'll find her in the place where we know not to go."

Aroha cleared a space for her in a spare bedroom. "Sleep, you're going to need it," she commanded, but that proved impossible. Renee lay awake through the night torturing herself, her mind filled with thoughts of what might be happening to Marika. Dawn saw her jittery with nerves and sleeplessness. Aroha, on the other hand, seemed unnaturally calm, cooking breakfast with little conversation and pushing a plate laden with bacon, fried eggs, baked beans and butter-soaked toast in front of Renee. She supervised Renee while she ate as if she were a child, ensuring she cleaned her plate, then left her to do god-knows-what while Renee paced and fidgeted and stared out the lounge window at the sea.

Aroha returned close to dusk in a battered ute, the bed of which was laden with assorted dive gear. "I had to ask around and borrow some extra stuff," she explained. "I don't normally go out on night dives."

They drove a short distance to a large storage shed where Aroha's own dive equipment was kept. Under Aroha's instruction, Renee loaded up wetsuits, tanks, fins and the like, while Aroha attached a small dinghy with an outboard motor to the ute's towbar. They drove in the direction Renee had come from the night before, only to veer off and follow a path alongside the trees until they reached the far end of the bush. A short, steep descent took them straight onto a large stretch of beach.

"You guys were just around there," Aroha pointed to the left.

They suited up in silence. The spare wetsuit belonged to Aroha's younger brother, and was a touch too big for Renee, but the belt adjusted snugly enough. With weights, torch, dive knife and spear gun attached, it felt heavier than she was accustomed to. They launched the dinghy and set off diagonally from the beach, angling towards the little bay where Marika was last seen, the boat's motor intrusively loud. After several minutes, Aroha shut it off.

"Best not advertise that we're coming," she whispered as she took up a set of oars.

Even the soft splash of the oars seemed too noisy for Renee. After perhaps half an hour, Aroha stopped and dropped an anchor.

"Just stick close behind me," she instructed. Then she was tipping backwards out of the dinghy. Renee did as she was told and followed hot on her heels.

Under normal circumstances, Renee would feel at home and at ease underwater; her love of diving was a partial influence on her decision to study marine biology. Tonight, though, the weight of the water made her claustrophobic, the darkness beyond her torch beam was ominous, and the muted sound of her own breath was panic-inducing. To calm her racing nerves she narrowed her focus, concentrating only on keeping Aroha's fins an arm's distance from her mask.

They followed a steady downward trajectory until they swam parallel to and a few metres above the seabed. Even to her experienced eye, the submarine terrain looked largely featureless, and she wondered what criteria Aroha was navigating by. Eventually Aroha stopped and turned to face her. She pointed down at what looked like a slab of rock flush with the sand, and gestured to Renee to follow her. Puzzled, Renee did so. As they drew closer, she saw through the optical illusion; there was a gap between the rock and the sea bottom, just high enough to admit the pair. They slowed their pace as they entered the gap and travelled along a narrow, rocky tunnel. Renee's anxiety mounted with every second.

The roof of the tunnel abruptly gave way to open water, and they finned up to find themselves in a large, air-filled cavern, the walls of which were daubed in an unidentifiable phosphorescence that gave off a dim, almost welcoming glow. They hauled themselves out of the water and shrugged off their tanks, masks, regulators and fins.

"God, it stinks in here!" Aroha held her hand over her mouth and nose and spoke in a whisper, yet her voice echoed off the walls. Renee shushed her, and pointed at the closer of two corridors that led from the cavern; it was as good a place as any to begin their search.

They tiptoed along the passageway, briefly inspecting the half dozen large rooms that opened off it. At a guess, Renee would have called them living quarters, furnished as they were with objects made of unrecognisable substances and not configured for human bodies. Thankfully, the rooms were devoid of life.

They retraced their steps and moved to the entrance of the second corridor. The stench was even stronger here, and Renee was almost overwhelmed by the instinct to turn tail and swim for her life away from the uncanny place, but a faint, distinctly human and distinctly feminine whimper overrode that impulse. She pushed past Aroha and ran down the corridor, her only conscious thought to follow the sound.

She found Marika at the end of the passageway in a cavern larger than the others. Her wife lay curled up on her side on top of a great stone slab positioned in the centre of the room. Except for the slab (there was something vaguely altar-like about it, which would make Marika the offering, a thought that Renee shunned from her mind the moment it arose), the room was empty. Here, the phosphorescent walls were overlaid with decoration, alien artworks that were at once exquisite and repellent. She didn't dare examine them too closely; just glimpsing them out of the corner of her eye made her head swim and her gorge rise.

Gingerly, as if she might disintegrate at any moment, Renee ran her hands over Marika's body. Her face was partially obscured by her hair, and she made no move to register Renee's presence, only continued her soft, plaintive whimpering. Her skin was slick with some clear, viscous substance. Renee sniffed at her fingers and recoiled, gagging; it reeked of the Ponaturi.

Aroha had caught up with her, and stood warily at the entrance to the cavern. "Is she okay?"

"She's alive," Renee replied. "No bleeding or broken bones that I can tell. But no, she's far from okay." She manoeuvred Marika to a sitting position, then onto her feet. When prompted, Marika moved willingly enough, but seemed completely without volition. Her eyes were wide and unfocused. It was if her mind and spirit had been drained from her, leaving only a beautiful shell.

They half-steered, half-carried Marika down the corridor, and were mere metres from the exit, when three Ponaturi stepped from another room to block their path. The two groups stared at each other for a couple of tense seconds, neither party expecting company. Then the Ponaturi charged.

Aroha, dive knife in hand and face twisted in fury, ran to meet them. All four tumbled back into the room from which the fish men had come.

Renee didn't wait to see the outcome. She dragged Marika past the melee, hauled on her dive gear faster than she would have thought possible, and jumped into the water with Marika in her arms, the cries of battle instantly muted as the brine closed over their heads. For one heart-stopping moment she thought that Marika's mind might be too damaged for her to know to hold her breath underwater, but that much of an instinct at least remained. Renee held her close and swam slowly, buddy-breathing all the way out through the underwater tunnel and back to the surface.

Mercifully, the dinghy had held on its anchor. Towing Marika's limp form through the water was one thing, getting her into the boat without capsizing was another much more difficult undertaking, and all the while Renee remained hyper-alert for signs of pursuit. After much dragging and cajoling, however, she had Marika stowed in a foetal ball in the bottom of the dinghy. With no further need for stealth, she powered the boat full throttle back to shore.

She did not speak of the events of that night. At first she felt guilty for abandoning Aroha, but soon she convinced herself that there had been no other way; Aroha knew better than she had what they were in for, had even warned her of the danger, and if she'd stopped to help, it would have only resulted in three women held captive in the Ponaturi's lair. Besides (the dark thought lurked), the way Marika had been flirting with Aroha, Renee felt ready to hand her over to the Ponaturi anyway.

For weeks afterwards she anticipated a knock on the door, a visit from authorities: we're investigating the disappearance of this woman, what can you tell us about that? But the visit never eventuated, and why would it? Most likely, someone in the family found the dinghy she'd abandoned on the beach, noticed the missing dive gear, and put some of the pieces of the puzzle together. They would have closed ranks and kept quiet.

They know. They all know…

Marika never emerged from her near-catatonic state, not even when she went into labour nine months later, so her baby boy was delivered by caesarean. Casual acquaintances assumed that Renee was the biological mother with the child conceived through fertility treatments, or that he was adopted, and that Marika's mysterious mind wipe was a tragic coincidence. Those closer, if they suspected the truth, did not pry.

The boy—Renee named him Matiu, the irony of which she did not discover until months later—was robustly healthy from birth, and hit all the right developmental milestones slightly ahead of schedule. Still, Renee could not help but wonder what might be developing in his half-alien mind. She hired a nanny to care for both mother and son while she worked, but none of them ever stayed for more than a month or two, and none could meet her eyes when they tendered their resignation. Perhaps it was the nauseating odour of rotting fish that clung to everything in the apartment no matter how thoroughly it was cleaned or what manner of perfumes were used to disguise it. Or perhaps it was Matiu's odd appearance that drove them away. He had none of his mother's good looks; his head was abnormally narrow, his eyes bulged unnaturally, his nose was so flat as to be almost non-existent, and his skin was peculiarly rough for such a young infant..

His strange looks certainly made her think equally strange and decidedly un-maternal thoughts. The thoughts were most intense when she was bathing him (and even bath time was weird, as he would only tolerate cold water with a full cup of salt added). With his spindly limbs giving off that smell, his unnerving, bug-eyed gaze fixed on hers, and with his mother sitting slack-jawed and staring at nothing, she often had the urge to put the pair of them in the car, drive them to the coast, and abandon them to the care of the creatures who had made them so.

Other times, the impulse was simpler, clearer, and more primal: maybe I should push his head under the water and hold him there. Just to see what will happen.

MEMORIES TO ASHES

PAUL MANNERING

I was three months shy of my sixteenth birthday on the night of 2nd April 1920, when the sky turned the colour of a deep bruise.

Late that afternoon the warm wind felt thick against my skin as I closed the front gate and walked to the house. Looking southward down the coast, into the teeth of the coming storm, I felt a chill sense of awe. Grey sheets of rain hung between the mountainous clouds and the slate dark sea. Now, more than ever, the air felt alive and the fading light pulsed with a strange energy. I inhaled and felt my skin tingle. With my hair blowing in all directions I went inside, leaving the rising storm howling like a dog.

"Half," Mother called from the kitchen. "Get the children bathed before tea."

Though I was christened Hannah, my family calls me Half, perhaps because I am the fifth child of ten and the eldest to survive past infancy. I came into this world the same way as my brothers and sisters, both living and dead, each of us born squalling and bloody on the bare wood of our kitchen table.

Home was a narrow strip of land between the sea and the mountains on the coast, north of the fishing village of Kaikoura. The mountains might one day be tamed for farmland, but not in my father's time. He survived by fishing in a small boat with my brothers, where they dragged nets and hauled lines. They fished only a hundred yards from shore, where the ocean turned black because the mountains did not end at the beach. The rocky peaks tumbled down to the true floor of the world miles below, and we lived on a ledge like limpets clinging in a tidal pool.

In summer, we swam the surface of the abyss; I remember feeling the beach drop away under my feet and the swirling cold tendrils of dark water twisting up from the ocean depths. We had childhood's innocence and our ignorance gave us courage.

I shared a room with my younger sister, Ruth, and our youngest brother, James. The older boys, Luke and Peter, had the other room. Aged eleven and thirteen they were decreed old enough to work with father on his fishing boat, or any other paid labour he could find in the Kaikoura district. The natural differences between boys and girls were no mystery to children growing up on a farm, yet I was glad to be away from the boys at night, to have a place where I could brush my hair, read and re-read the books I had managed to gather, all while dreaming the fanciful reveries of a young lady. This was my singular escape from the daily cycle of chores and housekeeping. As a girl of six, Ruth talked incessantly about nothing of consequence. James, at four, kept silent for the most part. He saved his voice for strident demands against his older brothers to wait for him to catch up when scrambling after them on their treks along the shore. As always, I brushed my hair and drifted in my reveries until Mother came in to remind me to go to bed.

The rain started close to midnight, when James was asleep and Ruth had crawled into my bed whimpering at the roar of the wind. I stroked her hair and shushed her gently until, in this warm and safe embrace, little Ruth slept like the freshly dead; warm and still. I lay in the still, close dark, feeling the house creak and groan under the tempest's onslaught.

In darkness memory's whispers come unbidden and insistent. Like Ebenezer Scrooge in Dickens' fabulous tale, I am visited by ghosts in the night. Mine are the shades of regret and shame and they bring no visions of the future, just an endless parade of historical guilt. They arrive astride the sharp-hoofed steeds of headaches, with which I am plagued without warning or mercy. I lie awake, the accused in a court of my own curation, where I sit in judgement and beg for execution. I know there are those with worse stories than mine, who suffer greater nightmares of despair, their minds and bodies warped by torment and abuse. I would pray for them, if I believed in a merciful God.

On other nights, my defence against the torment of night's solitude was to work hard during the day, driving myself to exhaustion so that sleep would come as inexorably as dawn. That night, long ago, under the cowl of the storm, the wind howling in discordant harmony reflected my own inner turmoil, and the pounding of pain's nails in my temples.

When James screamed, I sat up, my heart pounding and eyes wide, while Ruth merely whined and burrowed deeper into the warm mattress. James sat up with hair plastered across his face, his eyes glowing white in the darkness.

"Jamie?" I whispered.

My little brother stared at the opposite wall. I waited for him to fall back into sleep.

"Run…" The voice that rattled from Jamie's throat sounded rough and foreign.

"Jamie?" I swallowed and tried to breathe.

"Donovan! For God's sake run!" James screamed so loud that Ruth half-woke with a wail. From their bedroom I heard father curse and mother speak quickly to soothe him.

I clambered over Ruth as I rushed to James' cot.

"Jamie, wake up!"

Mother came hurrying into the room as I shook her youngest child.

"Half, what in God's name are you doing? Leave the child be!"

"Jamie's having a nightmare, mother."

"Jamie, love," Mother settled on the edge of the cot and cradled James against her breast. She pressed a dry hand against his forehead and tsked at the signs of fever.

"It is cast adrift…" Jamie whispered in a voice closer to his own. "It will rise again…and the stars will fall."

"Hush now Jamie." Mother rocked him gently until he subsided into quiet slumber again.

I didn't sleep again that night and was slow to rise at dawn. Now the storm had passed, leaving only grey, cold rain. Ruth slid out of my bed, her cotton nightdress—a hand-me-down that I wore when I was her age—sweeping the floor as she bustled to the distant bathroom.

"I had a bad dream." James mumbled from his cot.

"Did you now?" I spoke gently as it seemed clear that Jamie had only limited memory of his outburst.

"There was a monster and it killed everyone," Jamie intoned. I could see the memory of the nightmare fading in the morning light. It was the way of dreams; so vivid and real in the mind's eye at night, but slipping away like mist come dawn.

"Just a dream, Jamie," I reminded him.

"Nyah," he said and slipped out of bed to follow his sister to queue for the lavatory.

My first chore was to help mother make breakfast for the family. Growing boys ate their weight in porridge every morning, and would be begging for lunch before noon. After breakfast, father and his two young men departed with the horse and buggy for a farm further up the coast, where a day's paid labour was waiting for those with the strength for it. The atmosphere of the house was, as always, lighter once they had departed.

I set to cleaning and then mother tasked me with minding the children, which meant going to the beach to gather driftwood for the kitchen stove. The morning after a storm there are always new things to see and collect among the sea smoothed stones.

I dragged the wood-sled—easy enough when it was empty, a Herculean task when it was loaded with plunder—across the dirt track that, in later years, would be a tarsealed highway, and climbed the tussock-topped dunes. Our beach was a ridge of smooth stones, some as small as marbles, others as big as a fist. In the stories, beaches always had golden sand, but we had much younger earth. Close to shore we started picking up wood; storm-tossed branches, bleached and mummified by salt water. They would dry in the lean-to against the house and the larger pieces would be broken by father's axe. The kitchen stove had an endless appetite and I imagined it was a dragon, sleeping under the mountain with only its mouth showing and our hearth built around it.

I lifted my little brother to my hip, "Look Jamie, a forest has washed up overnight."

James frowned at the tangled branches and seaweed in all directions, some shadow of his nightmare still lingering around his eyes. "R'lyeh," he whispered.

"Who knows what treasures me might find?" I suggested to Ruth and set James down again. She had a magpie's eye for shiny things. After every trip to the beach, she brought home shells, shards of eroded glass and exotic stones with stripes and veins.

We selected the best wood, as large as each could carry. James, as usual, tried to lift wood bigger than he was, and Ruth found the distraction of coloured stones and pretty shells impossible to resist. The sled had half a load and the chill of the morning was gone from my bones when I fetched upon a twisted limb. I pulled it free from the tangle and it resisted. I pulled again, with half a mind to abandon it as there were other, easier logs to collect, and the driftwood shifted in my hands. A moan, unlike any sound I had ever heard, came from the storm-tossed pile.

I dragged a clump of thick brown kelp aside, thinking that some lost sheep had become trapped in the tangle of flotsam. As I considered calling Ruth and Jamie to share my find, I lifted more tendrils of kelp aside and found a man's boot. I held my shout in check.

I had never found a body on the beach, though father told of coming across a fisherman washed up dead, still tangled in his net, his exposed flesh eaten by the tiny sea-lice. I nudged the sailor's boot with my foot. There was weight to it, suggesting it contained a foot. My hand flew to my mouth as the boot moved of its own accord. With a quick glance to ensure the children were well away and occupied, I hurried to excavate my find.

With effort I heaved the haphazard cast of driftwood aside. Beneath, I found a man, face down and moaning as he grovelled with his hands and head, burrowing into the soft gravel.

"Sir?… Mister?" I wanted to reach out and touch him, to put a hand on his shoulder and tell him that he was safe from the sea and that the storm that had delivered him unto us. But there was a smell about the fellow, a stink beyond salt and despair, a stench reminiscent of an offal pit on a summer afternoon.

I stepped back and took up a discarded stick with which to poke him and gain his attention. I jabbed him at first tentatively, then with determination.

He cried out, squirming like a freshly landed fish until he turned onto his side and shielded his face with one filthy hand.

"Are you injured?" I know my tone sounded aloof. I might have been asking him if he wished for sugar in his tea. I could see his right foot impossibly twisted and the taut fabric of his trouser leg strained under the pressure of infected flesh.

"R'lyeh," he moaned. "Oh God… The stones are opening…it sees us!"

This being my first encounter with a true lunatic, I found myself at a loss on how to respond. "Should I fetch my father, sir?"

He sat up with a swift motion that startled me terribly. I readied my stick to thrash him should he prove violent. Instead he made an imploring gesture, "Water… Please, I beg you."

A gasp from behind told me that my discovery was no longer a secret. Young James peered from behind his older sister's dress, his thumb firmly in his mouth, his eyes wide.

"Ruth, take Jamie back to the house. Do not tell anyone of this until I have spoken to mother."

Ruth stared at the ragged figure with a morbid curiosity.

"Now please, Ruth."

She departed, leading her brother, who for once did not protest at having to hold her hand.

"What is your name?" I asked the destitute sailor. It felt like a grown-up question, one that father would ask if he were here.

"Pa…Parker…Joseph Parker," he whispered as if afraid his voice would be heard.

"Are you a fisherman, sir?"

"No such luck," he tried to laugh, and wheezed into a phlegmy cough instead. "I was crew on the *Emma*, out of Auckland."

"Were you wrecked in the storm last night?" I looked out to sea, searching for evidence of a ship, or other survivors.

"Storm? It was no storm." He tried to stand and his leg refused to take his weight. He fell heavily, cursing and muttering. "Water, damn you, water!"

"I will be back shortly."

I fled then, running over the dunes that marked the border between land and sea. Ruth and James of course dithered in the way of children given clear instruction, and I flew past them as I ran to the rainwater barrel next to the house. I filled the bucket and, struggling with the weight of it, I made my way back to the beach.

The man lay still, muttering to himself and responding to unheard voices.

"I have brought water," I said.

He jerked as if struck and then crawled to the bucket where he ducked his head and slurped the water like a pig at a trough.

My feelings of fear at his strangeness evaporated into pity and disgust. He was alive, and a living person has little of the dread majesty of a corpse.

"I will tell my mother you are here, she will know what to do with you."

Parker's face lifted from the bucket, his straggly beard and ragged fringe dripping water and catching the glint in his eyes as he stared at me.

"I see you, Hannah, the one they call Half. The better half long dead, I see. All that you hide. I see it."

My name was common enough and perhaps Ruth or James had said it within his earshot. The rest of his words were spiteful and uncouth, the sort of foulness to be expected from a rough sailor.

"Your leg is hurt. My father will be home soon, he will help you."

"You will tell no one—your father especially. You, who told the truth once before. You, who bears such scars. There is much I would tell you of elder dreams and formless seas. Of the infinite that draws breath but once an aeon, and the secrets of stars burned cold in ancient times."

"I don't understand…" my voice came from far away. In the

sunshine, I felt colder than I ever had.

"The babe died," he said, his words a statement of the inevitable. Words carved in stone as an eternal testament to shame. I wanted to run again at those words. Driven by a rising scream that came from the deep dark where memories are cast, that bottomless pit of the mind where things we wish to never think of again are exiled.

Parker continued, his voice a rasping sound that cut my resolve to ribbons. "Do you see it in your nightmares, a slug born in a torrent of blood and cramping pain? Not the usual monthly courses. No, this was anger and vengeance, the blood of shame and sin. You were bound in darkness, adrift on the dark sea, in the chasm of your depravity, the abyss of your mind. What did you see there, so deep, so dark? Did it drive you back towards the light?"

My feet were bound in the smooth gravel and I desperately wanted to run, to never hear this man's voice again. To run so far that memory and shame could never find me.

"You opened yourself to him, like a whore on the waterfront. Pale and shaking you drew him inside you. Burning with your desire and the power you held over him."

My throat went dry, binding my tongue to the roof of my mouth. I could barely breathe as his foul words fell like hammer blows.

"Words of love..." Parker sneered, snorted phlegm deep into his throat and then spat. Black-green and vile, I am sure the slime slithered of its own accord away from the light of the sun and into the cold comfort of the rounded beach pebbles.

"Shut...shut up." My arms were locked to my sides, numb as driftwood and unable to cover my ears against his litany of awful utterances.

"Did he seduce you, or did you pursue him? The haymaking season was nearing end, a celebration in the district. A church gathering with fine food, warm beer, and distilled spirit. Your head filled with romantic nonsense. One kiss and you fancied yourself in love."

My legs moved of their own accord, carrying me across the grinding surface of the pebble beach and onto the ancient dunes. I had abandoned the wood-sled, the bucket and my composure, running blind with tears streaming down my face. I fled past the house, setting the dogs barking from where they were tied under the pine trees. I ran around the vegetable garden and over the wire fence at the bottom of the hill. The scrub and bush on the steep slope were a place to hide. We played here often; filling the time between chores with complex story-games of knights and damsels, brave explorers and the mysterious natives of lost kingdoms. I threw myself down on the damp earthen floor of the hut my brothers had built in the bush. Swept away on an unstoppable torrent of sorrow and pain, I howled and wept until my stomach cramped. Curling into a ball, gasping and dry in my misery.

The devilry wrought by the strange sailor washed up on our beach terrified me. There had indeed been a young man, I had been in love, and to my eternal shame and despair I gave myself to him at the end of last summer's haymaking. When all the local families gathered around the white-board parish church to share and celebrate the end of a long month's work, my heart was lost in a swirl of romantic fantasy. He wooed with his sweet words. Nothing would have come of it, nothing but my shame. Our tryst would be a secret kept, as many are, until the confines of the grave allow it to finally return to the darkness of rot and hearsay. But my secret would not be so easily contained. At first, I gave little thought to the absence of my monthly cycle. It had been two months since that summer's in the manuka and ferns behind the church, and my heart's desire was fading, as I had not seen the young man since. Each morning I found myself rushing outside and retching thin bile into the dry, sandy soil. After the fourth such incident, I wiped my mouth and straightened, only for my heart to stop as I saw mother standing on the kitchen step, her arms folded and her face stony.

"You'll want some tea," was all she said.

I followed her indoors, meek and silent. She served tea, the black leaf from a store box, normally reserved for visitors.

"When did you last have your monthly, Hannah?" Mother asked.

I blushed deeply. Though matters of birth and death were an everyday occurrence in a farming community, to speak of menses was rare.

"I don't remember," I mumbled.

"You've not used your cloths in weeks," she said.

I looked up, surprised that mother would have noticed such a thing. I kept a handed-down supply of absorbent rags in a drawer in my room and had not imagined mother would have noted the pattern of their use.

"Who was it?" Mother had her back to me, standing at the stove, stirring the morning's porridge and giving no clue as to her expression or thoughts.

"I…" I did not dare betray him. My heart still held on to hope that he would come back and take me away to a new life where I would be his wife and we would live in comparative luxury.

"You will tell your father."

In all things my father had the authority and wrath of the Old Testament God. Mother's words were tantamount to an order of execution. I had been thrashed before for my daydreaming and other transgressions, though to be unwed and with child would be far beyond any wrongdoing in the history of my family. If I were not the one facing his unimaginable fury, I would have been fascinated to see what form his rage would take.

My nausea returned with a vengeance, and I fled to the garden to retch acid.

That evening father came home from the sea, only Peter old enough to aid him in drawing in the net. The catch had been poor and father's mood was as dark as the southern sky with an approaching storm. I waited until he had eaten his fill of supper and his second pipe load wreathed smoke through the kitchen.

"Father," I whispered.

"What is it Hannah?"

"Please…please forgive me," I felt the strength of prayer in my voice. I was beseeching an omnipotent figure to show me mercy after all.

"What are you mumbling about?"

"Father, I am going to have a baby." My words tumbled out in a flood. My confession pouring out in a gush, like the lifeblood from a slaughtered beast's throat. In its wake I was left pale and shaking.

"What?" father asked. "Helen!" he roared. My mother appeared from where she had been putting the children to bed.

"Yes?"

My father rose to his feet, his pipe falling to the floor, the embers of tobacco scattering on the boards. "Hannah…" was all he said.

My mother nodded, her hands clasped in front of her own belly. With my head bowed I watched her knuckles knead white against themselves.

"I only found out this morning," Mother said, absolving herself of any complicity in my crime.

"Who is the father?" my own father asked.

"She will not say," Mother accused.

"By God, Hannah. You will tell me his name!" Father's anger exploded out of him.

I shook, but whispered, "No."

My father took up the poker from beside the stove, a finger of iron as thick and long as my arm. I had often imagined it to be a rapier or enchanted sword for slaying dragons or evildoers that may invade our castle during my games.

Father raised it to his shoulder, his face darker than night, lips pinched thin in his fury. "Tell me his fucking name!"

Such a word had never been uttered in my presence before. To hear my father scream such profanity shook me to my core. I trembled and remained silent.

The half-remembered dreams that came to me that night were dark and wild. When I awoke in my bed, I remember being thirsty, my throat drier than the dirt track that ran past the house. I was as the ship of the Ancient Mariner; my boards had shrunk. So much so, that my body was skin and bone. Mother came into the room in response to my mewling. She hugged me, weeping tears onto my shoulder, and then she brought me thin soup. I was fed like a child, and after my famishment was absolved, I noted the small boy watching with large eyes from the doorway.

"Jamie," Mother said, "Come and see your sister, Hannah."

"Hello Jamie," I said, though I could barely speak through the remnants of sleep. He regarded me in fearful silence. I wondered why he seemed so uncertain.

"I have slept late, Mother," I started to apologise, and the words, came out, jumbled and malformed from my throat.

"You're alright now," Mother reassured me. "Your father will want to see you."

The fear in my eyes was apparent enough for mother to pat me gently on the shoulder. "He has forgiven you."

I did not know my father was capable of forgiveness. He had never expressed such sentiment in my hearing before, not for his fellow man, nor for the vagaries of fate and nature that he believed conspired against him in matters financial, and the gathering of provisions.

"I need to visit the lavatory," I went to leave my bed and found my legs in a weakened state.

I had no strength to refuse mother's aid and she tended me like a youngster struck with a winter fever; soup and bed rest, with no demand that I rise and complete my chores. Father, to my surprise, was almost affectionate that first evening after my confession.

During the month following that strange morning, my constitution slowly refreshed. No one in my family spoke of my sin, and when my cycle arrived with its customary inconvenience, the memory slipped into shadow.

This was when the blinding headaches made themselves known for the first time. Under their dark spell I would lose my sense of place and time, awakening on the beach, or down the track that led to town, with no memory of how I came to be there or the purpose of the errand that had sent me on the expedition. Mother, or one of my siblings would meet me on the return journey and, usually without comment, they would take my hand and we would walk home. Embarrassed that I had reneged on my chores, I would remain silent, and yet was never scolded.

I do not know how long I lay on the dirt floor of the hut in the bush. I dozed and daydreamed, my mind swept up in the vagaries of clouds, the myriad patterns in the sun-lit leaves, and the sharp-edged echo of the sailor's cruel words. Then, through the haze a shadow appeared. I wiped my face and blinked. "Jamie?"

"Hannah," he spoke with the voice of the little boy, though his eyes were dark like the storm. "Cthulhu fhtagn."

His meaningless utterance stabbed through me as though I was the boy, Kay, in Andersen's *Snow Queen,* and my heart was turning to ice.

"Ph'nglui mglw'nafh Cthulhu R'lyeh wgah'nagl fhtagn." Jamie intoned, his eyes rolled up in his head, the whites turned smoky grey.

My demand that Jamie cease this foolishness came out as a moan. I got to my knees, fists curling through the dirt. "James!"

The boy raised his thin arm, pointing towards the sea, "The sleeper awakens."

Jamie took my hand and marched down the hill towards the house. Mother stood in the dusty yard, Ruth tugging at her skirts and pointing at us as we climbed through the fence.

"Half!" Mother shouted. "What are you doing?"

"Mother! There's something wrong with Jamie!"

Mother's face twisted, "James, what is your fool sister doing?"

Jamie ignored her and continued his march towards the sea, dragging me with him, leaving mother and Ruth in our wake.

At the beach Parker had dragged limbs of driftwood together. I thought it was a strange pyre he was building, then it seemed to shift, as if twisting in the early evening's light, and I saw he had made an edifice like a door; a high and rectangular portal through which only darkness could be seen.

He paused in his work of cladding the structure with piled stones and squirmed around on his belly to stare at the two of us.

"The gate is prepared. The sleeper awakens! Ph'tagn! Cthulhu nyah!" Parker screamed to the sky.

Jamie tightened his grip on my hand, dragging me closer even as I dug my heels into the cold stones.

Parker clawed at his twisted leg, tearing the fabric of his trousers, exposing swollen and putrescent flesh. Gibbering, with spittle flecking his scruffy beard, the mad sailor seized the offending limb and pressed his broken nails into it. The skin ruptured under his burrowing fingertips, oozing foul pus. I moaned in horror as he tore chunks of his own muscle away from the bone.

With blood streaming from his hands and torn leg, Parker offered the chunks of himself up to the darkening sky. With a monstrous howl he cast the torn parts of himself upon the driftwood pile.

James tugged on my arm. "Look and see," he insisted.

The compulsion to raise my eyes and stare into the void beyond the door was irresistible. I squirmed, desperate to twist free of James' grip and cover my ears against the shrieking howls and demonic utterances spewing from Parker's throat even as my little brother pulled me closer to the edge.

The darkness beyond the door the lunatic had made now glowed like a mirror in a dark room, hoarding scraps of light and illuminating terrors. A figure waited in the dark reflection; both familiar and unsettling, a memory that beckoned. I reached the edge of the portal, extending my hands to grip the salt-dried wood of the frame to keep myself from plunging into the void. I gazed into the abyss and saw myself. My hair shone, my eyes were bright, and my face filled with the innocent certainty of youth. Then, as a cloud passes over the moon, the visage changed. I saw my father, his hand raised in fury, the iron poker striking down on my head. He beat me until mother lurched into the scene, desperately clawing and driving him away. I lay crushed and still, framed by blood as my mother wailed and cradled my limp form. The mist of memory swept over the scene and I lay in my bed, bandaged and asleep as the moon and sun fled through the sky, and the swell of my belly marked the quickening passage of time. I lay still, sleeping like the dead. The child came and I did not stir. No Sleeping Beauty awaiting the kiss of her prince, I lay and withered, tended by mother and fed through a yellow tube and glass bottle that hung over my bed.

The babe harvested from my womb squalled, and then crawled. He stood and walked while I lay in darkness. He was raised by his grandmother, and she called him James, her son.

"That which is not dead can eternal lie," James intoned at my side. I knew the truth of it then. I had lain on death's threshold for two years or more before awakening to confusion and loss of memory. The face I now saw reflected bore the scars of my father's fury, they tracked around the sunken eyes and hollowed cheeks of my long coma. I reached up and touched the softly unnatural depression in my skull where the bones had been crushed by the poker's blows. The sagging tilt of my eye, and the dull expression in my eyes, I was the Fool made flesh, older than I remembered, no longer a girl on the verge of womanhood. A cage of flesh and bone, my mind and soul alive and vibrant but my voice and visage muffled by the simpleton my father had made me.

My howl rose in shrieking harmony with that of the mad sailor as darker forms came forth from the emptiness where I had lain. They took shapes that did not materialise in measurable dimensions. These were timeless things, drawn here by the devotion of Parker and the siren call of my own presence between life and death with James, my child, formed as I lay in the half-dead void. We three were the catalyst: the lock, the key and the light that called them to our world. They were entities beyond human understanding, reaching for the door and gibbering in glorious salutation. Their deliverance was at hand.

I cried out and turned away from the insanity that whispered of an end to it all.

"Hannah!" the voice of my father, stricken with terror, pierced the rising tempest before me. I saw him running up the beach, returned from the sea, the hurricane lantern in his hand. "Hannah!"

"Father!" I cried out. Though now I heard the voice from my broken face. "Faghaahh!" Less human and more the inhuman dialect uttered by Parker in his madness.

The man who had nearly killed me for the shame of falling

pregnant out of wedlock swept me up in one strong arm. The other swung the steel and glass lantern as Parker struggled to his feet and lunged at us. The lamp shattered against the sailor's skull, drenching him in burning oil.

Parker fell back, arms flailing and the inferno engulfed him as he toppled against the altar he had made to the elder things.

My father cradled me. He wept as the burning man's tinder set alight the driftwood pyre. I stared into the flames and saw eyes as cold as distant stars staring back at me before the way was lost in consuming fire.

I know they will come again, when the way is opened. When the stars align. When death is denied and a child is born.

MASQUERADES

MARTY YOUNG

Tom Holland stopped in the middle of the gravel road, toying with the small ring in his pocket as he watched the man approach.

The narrow forestry road slipped on past the figure and disappeared around a small bend, taking the deformed pines and the giant tussock toetoe with it, but the man was suddenly central to that picture, the world framed around him. There was something in one of his hands. It looked like a book, or a brick. Whatever it was, it was heavy and threatened to unbalance him as he walked. Despite the weight of that object, his stumbling gait was more awkward and jerky than it should have been, almost like he was unaccustomed to being upright.

Tom tried to ignore the crazy thought even as it formed but it quickly stained his thinking with shadows, and those shadows were drawn towards the man, darkening the already black clothes that he wore. Worse still, was how that darkness seeped from his clothes to billow behind him like some kind of midnight cloak that tore along the ground.

Tom went to rub his eyes clear of his tired hallucination but he paused, his arms half raised. That cloak: there were shapes within it, twisted and broken and roiling like storm clouds, pulling back against his forward motion.

"Hell—" The cut-off word was loud but scratchy, forced up through a throat full of scabs.

"What..." Tom whispered, his voice running out. The dense native forest lurking beyond the wilding roadside pines was suffocating; sweat beaded across his brow and down his back. The sun was still high but hidden behind storm clouds, adding to the humidity. Yet a shiver streaked down his spine and his flesh broke out in goose bumps.

He heard sounds now, too, a swirling wind full of voices, all deep and animalistic, the words jagged angles that cut his hearing to make him wince:

'-fhtagn llllll-nglui-'

He backed up a step, glancing behind him. No one was in sight; only the bloody, deformed trees of what had once been the Maungataniwha Pine Forest. Many kilometres back, the gate that had locked off this once privately owned land from the public hung open and broken, the warning signs long since ignored and overgrown by the hordes that now came this way. He'd been surrounded by others as he trekked through the forest, men and women passing him in their hurry. Some would share a smile, a word, but not many. Most passed in silence, anxious for what lay ahead.

But now, somehow, he was alone with this stranger.

"Hello!"

The second effort was even worse than the first, sounding as if the word had drawn fresh blood from those throat wounds.

"Oh, get fucked," Tom croaked, wincing as the weird whispers continued to stab into his head.

'Y'ai 'ng'ngah, Yog-Sothoth h'ee-l'geb f'ai throdog uaaah-'

"Hello, friend," the figure giggled. It raised an arm with which to wave, but the gesture was all wrong. The whole limb wobbled bonelessly, the hand fixed at the extremity flopping like a caught fish.

Tom's legs almost gave out. He staggered himself this time in an effort to remain standing, stumbling away from the approaching nightmare. His vision narrowed to a sharp focus. But before he collapsed into screams, or turned and fled, the stranger called out and this time it was a very human sounding word.

"Hey."

Gone were the wet, wrong sounds and the sharp whispers,

and gone too was the cloak of shadows that flowed after the surreal figure.

"You don't want to come this way," the guy called as he closed the distance between them. "This is the last stop of salvation. Beyond here, our souls are in danger of disappearing into the darkness that masquerades as the light. Turn around, now, while you can!" He gestured with the small, thick book in his hand back the way Tom had come.

"I…I can't," Tom managed to say, shaking his head, trying to clear it of its confusion.

"But don't you know what's happening?"

Tom noticed the stained white collar tight about his neck, and the dust smearing his black outfit and turning his boots grey. He was an old man, a face all ridges and valleys, his dancing eyes more bloodshot than any iris colour. The remnants of his hair flapped about in the breeze, as if repulsed by the dark liver spots covering his scalp and desperate to escape.

"Tāne-mahuta has grown sick like his trees," the Father said. "His legs grow weak. It won't be long before he dies and the sky and earth come back together. Did you know gods could die?"

There was no evidence of the nightmare façade he'd seen before, but Tom raised his hands in peace and stepped past the Father, hurrying on, hoping he wouldn't turn and follow, but that's exactly what he did.

"Our gods aren't gods, not really. They're more than that, but much less, too. You're heading to Te Kore, aren't you?"

The void, the nothingness—only it wasn't nothing. It was everything instead, the ultimate chaotic reality.

"Leave me alone," said Tom, keeping a wary eye on the rambling man. And it *was* a man walking next to him, he told himself. Old and wrinkled and mad, but a man nonetheless. Stress had caused him to think otherwise. He was suffering how Mary had suffered in her last days, how she had suffered for so long.

"But you know it's not what they say it is. You're not another so easily fooled by wanton belief and desperation."

"Are they different? Wanton beliefs and desperation?"

"At one time I'd have said yes, without a doubt."

"But not anymore."

"It's already too late for you," said the Father, dejected. "The devil's got himself hooked on you well and good." He batted at his head. Two quick strikes, as if clearing away a spider web, or trying to catch the last of his hair. He went to rub his stubbled cheeks but discovered the book clutched in his hand. He held it out in front of him and stared at it as if he never expected to find it there. With a grunt of disgust, he tossed it to the ground, stumbling a step as he did so. "You've heard what they're saying?"

"What do you want? Please… Just…" He'd heard the stories, watched all the news footage. Trying to sort out for himself what to believe. What Mary must have believed, or wanted to believe. He stared at the bible the Father had thrown away. "Can't you just leave me alone?"

"The rhythms. They're all out of whack. That's what caused the false Gods to come, and now this Swiss cheese world of ours has lost itself. It's breaking further every day and there's little we can do about it."

Tom couldn't help but look off to the mutated trees lining each side of the road, the knobbly, pulsing growths covering their trunks, the branches that flexed and moved like tentacles rather than wood. And every so often there'd be a weird, high-pitched trilling sound that would bounce through the forest like incessant birdcalls. But there were no birds here, and he didn't know what could make such a sound.

Strange plants poked up from the leaf litter, odd violent shades of red and green that caused his head to ache whenever he looked at them. Even the drooping, plume-like flowers of the native toetoe in front of the pines writhed as though in twisted agony, their colours changing from the usual white to a vibrant, pulsing orange.

Whole towns, Te Pohue immediately south, Tutira, Putorino, and Raupunga, all the way to the coast of Hawke's Bay to the southeast, where oceanic things had been stirring and slithering up out of the depths to die on the sand, worshipped by strange cults that had gathered there. Even the shores of Lake Taupo, eighty kilometres to the northwest. All had felt the impact of what had happened.

"People still refuse to believe," the Father went on, staring at him, not needing his input for conversation. "Those who haven't witnessed the madness themselves find it easier to disbelieve, don't they? All fake news and propaganda. Because that would be accepting there was more, and that's too much to accept."

"Father," Tom repeated. "Please. I don't want any trouble. I don't believe in your God. I—"

Don't know what to believe, he finished silently.

He had walked for hours and his legs ached, his head pounded, and the chafing between his legs was getting worse. He wanted to curl up and be done with it, but he would reach Te Kore if it were all he could do.

And then he would know.

He increased his pace but so too did the Father, and for a moment the tread of their synchronised steps was the only sound in the newly alien world. There were no crickets to chirrup, or cicadas to trill. The forest lay poised about them, awaiting more. Hungry for more.

They walked, and the silence continued. The humidity grew, and Tom sweated. He kept glancing at the Father, waiting, expecting…what? He wasn't sure, but all he saw were deep lines at the edges of tormented eyes, and sallow skin. In side profile, the man's hunch was pronounced and Tom wondered how much it would take for him to fall over.

He was about to turn to the Father and demand an answer when the Father said:

"I had a congregation that came out here. They wanted to visit it, to see the miracle for themselves. A pilgrimage for the soul, they said. I told them not to, I warned them not to, but how could they resist? Moths to a flame."

Suddenly Tom understood. He'd heard that story; it was what had drawn Mary here.

"Twenty-seven of them. Men, women, and children," said Father James of the Raupunga Orthodox Church, known as the man in the photograph on the front page of newspapers, lying curled up in the forest, sobbing, silhouetted by brightness. "My flock. I failed them all. I should have stopped them. I should've known better."

Tom shrugged.

"Do you remember? They tried to block off the first one but the Church wouldn't let them, not this holiest of miracles. I wish the horrors had come sooner, before the Church had succeeded."

"Urbino," Tom whispered, remembering but not wanting to.

The Father laughed a bitter laugh. "The second coming, they called it. I guess it was, in a way."

Mad cults claimed they had summoned the Great Old Ones from the depths of the universe and returned them to Earth where they belonged. Other groups said what the Father had alluded to, that mankind had broken Earth's natural rhythms with our technological advances, and that disharmonious discord had torn open the fabric of our reality to let through nightmares. Yet more said it was nothing anyone had done, simply that the time was right and we were irrelevant in the overall scheme of things.

Regardless, too many doorways had opened all over the world, and the world lay ruined, forever ruined. The miracle had quickly turned to horror.

"Why are you heading there?" The Father suddenly glared at him.

"I told you, it's none of your business." Tom stared into the distance, imagining that the light he'd eventually find was already brightening the horizon. Would he be able to see it from here?

"You don't even know where it goes."

"Isn't that the core to faith? You believe what you want to believe and hold onto that with all of your heart, knowing it to be true, no matter what?"

"But don't you see?" Father James spun and grabbed Tom by his shoulder, making them both stop. "We're being fools. Never has faith led us in such blind ignorance! There are laughing demons and delighting devils waiting in that light. Mouths wide open ready to swallow us whole!"

"Get off me!"

"They thought our gods had come down from the skies to visit us, Puanga in the constellation of Orion, even Sirius, Rehua, eater of men from the highest of the skies, but we were misled. These, these, aliens are not our gods. They're corrupt beings. Tipua, supernatural monsters! They offer no salvation!" The Father grabbed Tom's arm. "I couldn't save them but I can save you. I can't let you do this!"

The heavy clouds and swirling winds that had risen as they walked created enough disturbed light to show Tom the truth again, to let him see what had hold of him. In place of hair was bone, cracked and splintered, and the sickly light gleamed upon moisture oozing from those fractures. The clothes sliding over its emaciated body were stained with old blood, and as torn as the face it wore.

"Friend—" It said, flashing teeth.

Tom screamed at the sudden sight.

Its face slid over its own hidden features like a rubbery mask, but this human mask did not fit, the eyes were empty holes, the nose dangled and bobbed, the mouth permanently open with the pocket of skin forming the jaw empty of bone and hanging down to sway with the creature's step. Beneath this human façade was something not yet clear for Tom to see, something that resembled the shifting forms behind it, whispers of features with no real definition. Something he had no desire to see with any clarity.

The distended shapes within the swirling cloak of darkness whipped about in a frenzy, excited at what was happening, throwing up gravel and dust alike. They screamed out but from such a distance that their guttural words remained indecipherable.

'R'luhhor mgepah, r'luhhor ah, ng r'luhhor ahor ah—'

Tom's cry failed but his mouth continued to move. He shoved at the thing that had pretended to be Father James, sending it staggering backwards, but it didn't let go, and Tom went with it. He jerked free before he fell into its embrace.

"Friend, do not...do not run—" It giggled, extending a violated arm in a parody of warmth. The holes it wore as eyes were without emotion.

The midnight cloak broke apart, sending obscure shapes out into the forest in a tidal wave, where they then rose from the ground and pushed back through the trees and ferns and toetoe until they crowded up against the road. Terrible, indescribable things, shapeless conglomerations of protoplasmic pustules, glowing with a sickly yellow internal light. There was the suggestion of eyes, horrible gleaming, staring eyes, too many to count. Eyes that were human and so many others that were not.

Tom lashed out, catching the Father, monster, demon or devil, across the face. He hit the fiend again, and a third time, each a solid punch to the slippery face, the right cheek, and all the time screaming, "Mary's there! She's in there and you can't have her! None of you can have her!"

Father James fell over backwards and his head hit the ground with a dull thud, a sound to make Tom gasp. The Father's arms and legs, which had flopped about him as he'd tumbled, went still, as did the world around them; a sudden, shocking stillness.

Tom's panic was the only thing to penetrate that silence, a heartbeat broken and running askew, ragged breaths of the sinful. Gone were the nightmare sights, the demonic visions. Even the presence of oppressive terror had passed, as if whatever had borne down upon him had now passed him over. All that lay in front of him was a beaten old man of the cloth.

Tom moaned, then covered his mouth with his hands, scared the land would announce his deed, pass it onto the wind and the trees to take to the authorities, who were far from here.

He fled. He thrust one hand deep into his pocket and pulled out the ring he'd given Mary on their wedding day and clutched it to his chest. He glanced back as he ran, although he didn't know if he expected the Father to be rising from the road, or if the sirens would be coming for him.

All he saw was the lump of broken humanity, and he stopped glancing back. He looked towards the glow he was certain he could now see ahead of him. His panting breath was filling with sobs, his vision blurring with tears.

"I'm sorry," he cried to Mary. "I didn't, didn't mean for that to happen. But he was…he wasn't human!"

His words ran out for they did nothing to appease his guilt.

Even surrounded by vegetation he couldn't explain, and enduring sights that threatened madness, Tom fought against acceptance of the new reality. It was too much.

The Father was right.

Loneliness and despair had driven him here, out to Te Kore as it was locally known, and he knew all too well how vile such emotions could be and what they could do to someone. Surely that was a more likely explanation?

But his mind swam with possibilities, the wild, insane tales that filled the news.

Countless millions had travelled to the original site when it had first ruptured, and when there had been no more room, they had sought other so-called thin places where the veil between realities was thinnest—St. Peter's Basilica in the Vatican City, the Blue Mosque in Istanbul, St. Patrick's Cathedral in New York, Bangla Sahib Gurdwara in New Delhi.

In the days leading up to the paganist Samhain, desperate flocks hoping that narrowness between worlds would help them traverse the boundary and find Nirvana, waiting for the midnight culmination of the Pleiades, built to crushing weights at these sacred sites, but all to no avail. The doors, when they opened, had done so randomly.

The clouds were thickening as he hurried on, darkening, dimming the light, and the shadows expanding, deepening, and becoming their own doorways.

He struggled to catch his breath but the shadows felt wrong, distended and infinite, dragging him into impossible worlds that broke apart his thoughts as though they were never meant for such places. Further back from the road, the darkness stirred, but the trees weren't moving and he couldn't feel any draft.

That sense of motion increased, getting closer.

He grasped the ring as this ancient land swelled about him. Ghostly hands tugged at his clothes and tried to drag him into the forest, fingers curled in his hair. Ahead, demonic figures stood waiting for him but wafted away as he came close; and then, amidst the trees, he saw gigantic faces, skeletal, stretched, with eye sockets filled with stars and mouths with grinning teeth. They all watched as he went past. Some slipped from those trees to fall in behind him, their gaunt forms of tangled limbs slow on the gravel road, in mockery of his stumbling walk.

Tom moaned again. He whimpered and began sobbing. He tripped over his feet, tumbling towards the bushes, where ghastly figures delighted in his approach. He cried out and arrested his fall, wobbling back into the middle of the road. He glanced around and saw a horde of impossibility following in his wake. His scream pierced the shadows and tore apart the trees, but the night stitched itself back together again even as he ran out of breath.

He fled, no longer looking back, unable to accept that sight, but expecting them to reach for him, to grasp him, devour him. Having been ignored, those wretched shapes surged up alongside him, festering undefined figures made of the rotten newborn night. He shut his eyes, gripping the ring tight, so tight it was imprinting upon his palm. It was hot too, burning him.

After several seconds, he opened his eyes, terrified of walking off the road. The entities were gone and he felt suddenly sick in their absence. Even behind him, the way was clear. He rushed onwards, giddy with relief as the burning ring went cool in his hand.

As he rounded a slight bend, he saw a small group of people on the roadside, ambling towards him but so deep in conversation that none of them had seen him. His first instinct was to cry out in delight and run towards them, but a ghastly thought caught him. He stopped, backing up until they passed from sight again, taken by the gradual bend in the road that had first revealed them.

Only then did his pace begin to slow, his every step weighted with monstrous guilt until he so resembled the Father's crippled walk. Unable to go on, he bent over, his hands on his knees, keeping his mouth shut so he wouldn't burst into screams.

A second passed, and it was an eternity. He gave himself longer, seeking control again. Hoping his trembling would pass, hoping to make sense of what was happening.

He heard them, up ahead, faint voices talking among themselves.

They'd pass him and find the Father.

But what would they do? Did such crimes have relevance anymore? Would they mete out their own justice, eager for the chance to flex their muscles?

Another question burned into his trembling thoughts; *why* were they coming this way, when everyone else was heading to Te Kore?

A frightening answer struck him as quickly as the question had come, making him think of the Father again, and the sights he'd seen.

"I don't know," he muttered. "I don't know! Oh Jesus, Mary, I don't know what to do!"

He clapped a hand over his mouth, but his sin continued to scream within.

He had attacked the Father and left him there to die. The man hadn't tried to hurt him; he'd tried to stop what he considered suicide. There'd been a monster there, all right, but it hadn't been the Father. It had been his own mind that had given him the excuse to do what he'd done. His poisoned imagination, rotted with pain and loneliness.

He had to return. He had to; how could he go on, knowing what he had left back there? How could he reach salvation with that sin tattooed onto his soul?

Mary would never accept him.

Unless what he'd seen…

He opened his hand and stared at the wedding ring, seeing Mary's happiness on that day so long ago, but she wasn't happy anymore. The smile that had captivated him was lost, replaced with condemnation, and sadness, too.

He moaned at the deformed memory and closed his fingers around the ring. She had always smiled at him from there; she'd guided him through his darkness, his light, leading him to safety despite the nightmares that had come in her wake.

But he had let her down. Seen madness where there hadn't been any.

"No," he said between tears. "I'll make this right, Mary. I promise." With a quick glance back to where that group would soon appear, Tom straightened and replaced the ring back in his pocket.

He looked back down the road and his heart lurched.

"Have to," he muttered, thinking of the hungry forest. Was that just more madness?

As he began retracing his steps, the shadows grew smaller, shallower, and the suggestive movement inside those shadowed pits stilled. He kept far from them, not trusting their laziness. Once, he heard words in the air, weird distant chanting that jarred his brain and curled his stomach. Words that made no sense but carried such an oppressive and ancient weight that they made him reel. He stumbled towards the ruined trees and fetid toetoe, and they surged out from their languid state and stretched out for him, almost clasping. Tom shrieked and jerked back.

'C' ah kadishtu ot mgahehyee nilgh'rishuggoggg—'

The chanting faded away and didn't come again.

He shrank within himself as he walked, hoping no one or nothing would pay him any further heed.

From one hundred feet, the Father was an indistinct shape, without humanity. A wart upon the road, and there were many such things now. Would one more matter?

Yes. It mattered more now than ever before.

The trees were settling, the native grasses and ferns growing still. Even the light was improving. The charged feel of the air had dissipated, the thrumming that vibrated within his soul and told him he was on the cusp of the infinite. He was left with mutated, near dead-looking trees and endless toetoe, and the rank humidity, as oppressive as ever but almost natural in its oppression.

When he reached the Father, he dropped to his knees and checked for a pulse. It was there, weak but there, and with that, Tom sobbed with relief. There was a lot of blood, most of it from the back of his head where it had collided with the bigger rocks near the edge of the road, but his cheek was split badly, too.

"Father?" He whispered, but the man didn't stir.

Unable to stop himself, he pressed a finger against the skin below the Father's split cheek. Panic flared within him and he staggered away.

"What do I do?" He asked the world. "Oh Mary, what have I done?"

He didn't have a phone and couldn't carry the unconscious man anywhere for help. Even if he could, did he want to, after what he'd done?

He looked in the direction Te Kore awaited, and thought of his wife, waiting for him there.

Soon after the group from the Raupunga Orthodox Church had made their pilgrimage, she had pressed her wedding ring into his hand and kissed him goodbye, slowing long enough to wipe the tears from his cheeks before leaving the house and closing the front door behind her.

There had been a taxi waiting to take her as far as possible towards her destination. It had sat there while they'd argued; him begging her *no*, and she telling him she couldn't go on anymore. Her depression had been getting worse and Mary had spent three months last year in hospital, barely caring enough to eat during that time. She couldn't take any more of the greyness, she'd said. It was slowly devouring her. She needed the light, and the happiness it entailed. She needed her own salvation.

And wasn't that where Te Kore led?

He had wanted to join her but she had said no. "You still have colour in your world, even without me. But I'm grey, flat. I know I love you, I know that somewhere deep within me, but I just can't reach that feeling anymore."

"You are the colour in my world," he'd said, but it hadn't reached her, either. Or if it had, she hadn't let on.

Tom bowed his head.

The New Zealand Defence Force had made a token effort to isolate Te Kore when it had first been discovered. Before the madness had come through.

The local iwi had helped, doing everything they could to protect their lands from the trespassers that came in droves, but soon it wasn't just words that leaked out from the rugged forests. There were gods let loose, gods they didn't know and had no room for in their pantheon. From neither their heavens nor their hells, these chaotic gods brought with them madness and despair, and they drove off the iwi and the military alike.

Mammoth forms now stole thought the night, rippling reality as they went. Disjointed sights and sounds to terrorize the heart had reached south to the capital of Wellington, and far north to Auckland. There were no signs of them stopping there, either. It was the same in Asia, and Europe too. The States, Africa, even Antarctica had broken open.

Voices from up the road stole into his despair.

There was one thing to do, but he was running out of time to do it. He took a deep, steadying breath, and returned to the Father, crouching in front him. Pulling out Mary's wedding ring, he placed it in the Father's front pocket.

Mary would understand. She knew all about sacrifices.

Her depression had meant they'd had to give up on their dreams of having children, so he had centred his life around her instead, being her rock when she needed him, even as she had spiralled inwards.

Whether he believed in Te Kore or not, it no longer mattered. This was where she'd come, so this was where he had to go. She was all he had.

"This will keep you safe," he whispered to the Father. "I'm… I'm sorry for what I did."

Then Tom rolled Father James off the road, grunting with effort and praying to his lost God for forgiveness, or at least understanding. The Father would be all right. He'd come to, and have a headache, but he'd be fine. And by then, Tom would be gone.

But as he committed this deed, the toetoe closest broke into movement, reaching out for the body. Tom leapt back, falling over, rolling and scrabbling away on his haunches.

The pulsing orange flowers surged in brightness as the toetoe pulled the Father into its fold.

"No," Tom yelled, clambering back to the Father, whose eyes had opened wide, his mouth doing the same in a silent scream.

Father James saw him and one hand, the one not yet devoured by the writhing plant, stretched out towards him. Tom reached for it, but then caught himself. Slowly, and with horror, he pulled his hand back, then closed his eyes and let his hand fall to his side.

In that internal darkness, Tom heard the slow, insidious rustle as the plant took in the sacrifice, and a single, solitary moan from the Father that made him flinch.

Tom kept his eyes closed until the sounds had ceased. When he reopened them, Father James was gone. He opened his mouth to cry, to moan, or wail, but there was nothing. He felt numb.

What had he done? Oh Jesus…

The light began to darken, the pretend night falling into place about him, congealing and going sour, great clumps of the night falling to the ground and leaking black to further spread across the landscape. Strange, glowing orbs formed out amongst the trees, merging into a pulsing mass of vibrant colours, before breaking apart again and drifting off into the coagulating darkness, re-emerging and growing together once more. The size of the entity was impossible to gauge; it filled the forest, extending upwards in more directions than possible, shimmering out of this reality and continuing elsewhere. It was endless, impossibly endless.

And there, on the edge of its existence in this plane, Tom saw a gigantic three-lobed eye staring down at him.

He felt opened up right to his insignificant soul, and deeper, down to every molecule of his sinful being. The feeling lasted mere seconds, and then that surreal eye discarded him, judgement complete, and the colourful orbs broke apart one last time and vanished, leaving a writhing suggestion of yellowish tendrils composed of shadows in its wake, before they, too, were gone.

"No, no, please." Tom babbled, reaching out to where it had been, pleading for it to take his hand, and, seeing the Father instead, reaching out for his. Then Tom was left with the twisted forest and its polluted shadows. A high-pitched trill sounded in the distance, and the trees echoed that cry.

Movement caught his attention and he saw a solitary figure standing on the road. The figure was tall, skinny and dark-skinned, wearing odd clothes, an old black suit of some kind, dusty and stained, with a red waistcoat.

"Father!" Tom cried out with joy, before realising it was someone else entirely. He screeched and scuttled away like a broken crab as shining, shimmering eyes violated him. The figure grinned and its teeth shone as brightly as its eyes, making Tom's vision spin, a whirlwind that threatened to engulf him.

A voice came to him amidst his terror and insanity, a deep sounding whisper that rent the remainder of his soul with the screams of nightmares; 'the stars await outside…'

He screamed for Mary; he'd held her tight so many times when he'd been trying to banish the darkness that was swallowing her. This time he needed sheltering, but he couldn't find her. He tried shutting his eyes so he could see her but terror wouldn't let him.

Somewhere in between those rapid blinks, the roadside figure vanished.

Then Mary was there. She was crying, tears causing her whole image to shimmer. He didn't dare wipe away his own tears because he knew that's where she existed, but she was fading as he watched, and he cried out for her, spiralling into a silent lonesome darkness where even his screams didn't penetrate.

No longer could he hear the group that had been approaching, nor the rustle of the hungry forest.

There was nothing.

He scrambled to his feet and started running to where he'd last seen them, his pace picking up until he was sprinting. But they were gone.

His anguish, when it came, was a howl, a deep, racking scream of madness and terror.

He searched his pocket for Mary's ring but it wasn't there. It wasn't in his other pocket, either. All that was left was a faint impression on the palm of his hand, even now fading out.

He felt emptied, scoured clean, lost within a dark void, and he finally understood Te Kore.

EDWARD'S JOURNAL

LEE MURRAY

I accept the package with trembling hands. Wrapped in brown paper and secured with string, my name is written in black letters on the front, the Y in Hennessey smudged at the top. I don't open it immediately, laying it on the sideboard while I go about my chores. Only when they're completed, do I gather up the package and take it into the garden to open away from the busy eyes of my sisters.

I sit on the bench seat facing the lane, where the scent of honeysuckle permeates the air, and prise open the knot to fold back the brown paper. My breath catches. There, on my lap, is Edward's journal, its brown leather cover stained and its pages warped and dog-eared. A dull ache settles in between my shoulder blades.

It's been thirteen years since I last saw it, the day he departed with the 57th regiment.

"Every man should have an adventure," he'd told me, his grey eyes twinkling with merriment as he lifted me off my feet and hugged me goodbye. It hadn't been proper – I'd been barely fourteen – but being my father's favourite has its benefits, and he had indulged us by looking away.

A swallow flits by, venturing out from its nest beneath the soffit. I watch it go, not ready to open the journal yet. Instead, I pull the crumpled letter from the pocket of my skirt, smoothing the paper out, and read every word, although by now I know them better than my heart.

January 1861.

Margaret, we are arrived this morning in New Zealand and await aboard for our orders. I admit to feeling no remorse at the prospect of leaving the Castilian, as I am no sailor. I do not know any among us who appreciated the incessant sway of the hull, the accursed creaking that robbed us of our rest, and the resolve of the cook to bore us senseless with the blandness of his fare. From where I write here on the deck, the port looks like any you would see in England, fertile and full of promise, although they say the terrain is deadly, and the natives, even our allies, are tricky devils. I do not say this to alarm you, darling Margaret, only to assure you that after our experiences in India, we of the 57th regiment are prepared for any challenge. If the Government wish us to enforce the peaceful settlement of these shores for God-fearing citizens, then we shall certainly oblige them. I shall not complain about the weather though, which, while warm, is pleasantly cooler than Bombay…

I smile again, remembering how Edward had never liked the heat.

Margaret, we were marched from the creaking timbers of the Castilian to a place called Onehunga, which the locals pronounce Own-nay-hunger. A risible name, and a risible tale, since not hours after we arrived there, we were made to board another ship, the warship HMS Cordelia, from whence I am writing, in spite of the swell of the ocean beneath me. As I pen this, we approach Waitara near New Plymouth, and the start of our next colonial adventure. I am invigorated by the prospect. Already, I can see the mountain that towers over this region, a perfect cone arising from the peninsula; this glorious edifice is surely a beacon to the gods. If there is time, I shall put this letter with the Quartermaster to despatch on his return to Auckland. I send all my best wishes to you, cousin, and to my uncle, your father.

Ever yours, Eddie.

I hold the letter to my face and inhale deeply, hoping for a hint of him, or perchance a vestige of the ocean. Any such trace is long gone and instead I breathe in the lilac I use to scent my own clothes. This letter: the last to reach me, written on pages torn from his journal. Six years, I've waited in vain for another. Since then, there's been nothing but rumour, each one grinding away at my resolve, stripping me of hope. Had he been separated from his regiment? Could he be lost in that alien forest, turning in circles, unable to find his way? Perhaps he died in battle and lay buried under the mud somewhere, his bones slowly rotting while strange plants sprung forth to conceal his resting place. Certain mean-spirited souls whispered behind my back that Edward had been a coward who ran from a fight and was now too ashamed to return. They said he'd forsaken me, choosing instead to take a native to wife and live with her like a savage in the bush. Ignoring the eyes that slid away from mine, I paid no heed to the ugly gossip that drifted in my wake and, after a while with no news to confirm or deny their validity, the rumours had stopped.

A year later, Arthur Bearnsley had come courting. A decent, gentle man with a good position, Arthur had been patient with me, but Edward was always in my thoughts. I kept him waiting too long for my answer, and, in the end, pressured by his mother, he wed another.

No fretting over shed milk, Margaret.

I allow myself the luxury of a sigh, then, wiping my eyes with the corner of my apron, I tuck the letter back in my pocket. What would his journal reveal? I run my palms over the warm leather, dallying. It's strange: all these years I've longed for news of Edward, now that I have his testimony in my hands, I'm afraid to open it. I do it quickly, selecting an entry at random.

4 April, 1864.

Margaret, I regret the poverty of my hand today, so childish I can scarce read my own words. In truth, I am trembling like a child. There are ten of us, separated from the first grenadiers. We are hidden in the bush after witnessing the very worst of humanity. I fear sharing this account with you, dear cousin, but we have always been frank, and if the words are too gruesome when I have completed the tale, as they surely must be, then I shall rip the pages from my journal and bury them in the scrub, for we cannot risk a fire…

We left early this morn from the redoubt at Kaitake. Taking the South Road, we were so buoyed with confidence and bravado, it is hard to fathom our departure was but hours ago. We were led by a man named Captain Thomas Lloyd. Our mission, the same as it has been for some time now, to burn or confiscate any crops and foodstuffs, which might sustain the Māori. We were to badger the natives into moving off the land and going elsewhere, wherever that may be. The day was nothing unusual: fresh and misty with a tang to the air. Lloyd split the party in two near Te Ahauhu. I remained with the captain's party. I was pleased to do it. A tall-ish fellow still with a good head of hair and fashionable sideburns that conflated his beard, the captain impressed me as a decent sort, solid and fair, and perhaps not as impetuous as some others of his age.

Margaret, I am stricken: Lloyd was cut down in his prime. It was only by Providence that I was not with him, as I had needed a moment of privacy.

Those cunning Hau Hau, the so-called Christian Māori, had built a trench system, cutting their saps deep into the bank, invisible from Captain Lloyd and his party ascending the slope. The rebels leapt from the trenches, ambushing our front guard. One of their warriors, a fearsome man with scars across his chest, lifted his club and with a single slice of that deadly blade, the captain's head was severed from his shoulders. Lloyd's white breeches did nothing to diminish the sight of his lifeblood pumping from that gruesome stump. There was so much blood, a river of treachery. Yet even in death, our noble Captain Lloyd fought on, his body twitching long moments on the ground.

In that instant, I avow, I did not go to my commander's aid. I was paralysed with fear. What advantage would there be in my dying too? So I stayed out of sight, and bit my hand to prevent myself from crying out. It was well I did. Seven soldiers were killed. Decapitated. Dooley lost a leg, cleaved off with one of those flattened greenstone blades. That isn't the worst of it. Like vampires, the Māori warriors drank the blood of our comrades. I watched while Eastman, Dooley and Poole were exsanguinated, their blood drenching the warrior's bodies. It drooled from the side of the warrior's mouths and spilled over their chests.

Not an Enfield was fired. No word was spoken. When the Hau Hau departed carrying the heads of our countrymen, the ten of us fled, bashing our way through the forest and into the hills.

My heart pounds, my chest tight with fear. Does he still live? I flick forward several pages, not to read them but to reassure myself that Edward had not perished that very night, perhaps overcome by the same Māori savages who had butchered his captain. To my relief, there are several more entries, somewhat rushed, but all written in Edward's familiar hand. Quieted, I return to the previous entry and, turning the page, continue my reading.

12 April, 1864.

Margaret, since Lloyd's demise we remain hidden in the foothills, isolated from our compatriots, awaiting reinforcement, which must surely come soon. We are only eight now, two of our number killed when we attempted to return to the redoubt the day after Lloyd's death. Setting out before dawn, we travelled single file through the grey bush, silent but for the thud of our boots on the mud, and the brush of ferns on our shoulders.

Not one saw who attacked us, or even the hour they attacked, but when we stopped to rest, Jones and Gilardy were missing. We retraced our steps, anticipating a mishap. It was a strong probability: the terrain is treacherous here, dense and dripping and full of unseen perils. A mile behind us, we found their boot marks, deep gouges scrapped in the mud and moss sloughed off fallen branches where they had been dragged through the undergrowth.

By now, Baxter had worked himself into a lather. His eyes wild, he said the men were lost, carried off by the murderous Hau Hau.

That fool, Grey, expects us to treat the Māori as our brothers, he railed. These thick-lipped people, who carve their bodies with chisels and knives and adorn themselves with crude ungodly patterns. How can we trust savages such as these?

McKenzie had scowled at that. It is widely known he is a sympathiser. The man keeps a native 'wife', even speaks the language. Under the circumstances, it was well he did not voice his viewpoint because Baxter was not alone in his belief that the Hau Hau had returned to slaughter us while we were weakened in both spirit and numbers. Uneasy, the men murmured and shifted their feet.

Does no one else smell a rat? Baxter warned us. He said we should go back. This piteous trail will only expose us to the same fate as our compatriots, he insisted. We should make for the redoubt.

He turned to go, but Finnigan and Ilot wouldn't have it. They don't call us the Die Hards because we turn our back on our own, Finnigan said, his finger raised like my old governor. Burly and thickset, Finnigan stands as high as a stallion with the muscles to match. It takes a brave man to stand up to Finnigan.

Baxter persisted. We ran when they killed Lloyd, he said.

That was different, said Finnigan.

Since Finnigan saved my life in India, what choice did I have but to agree? We set off, following the trail of desperate scuffs, Baxter reluctantly falling in behind us. Finnigan took the lead, cutting a trail through the trees as those calamitous tracks took us deeper and deeper into the forest. At times, the foliage was so dense and the mist so thick we could barely see in front of our faces, still, we pushed on. Then, without precedent, the scuffs stopped. Finnigan had us search the area for the men. With the dusk descending upon us we checked every embankment, lifted every fern. Margaret, we scoured every inch, we found not a trace of them.

The Hau Hau have them, Donaldson asserted.

We others could offer no more plausible explanation. Gilardy and Jones were lost. Even Finnigan was forced to admit it. Worse, in searching for the missing men, we'd lost our way, like Grimms' tale of Hänsel und Grethel. Ilot disagreed, assuring us that all was well, that if we kept our current course, we would meet the trail again, that we might yet encounter the garrison search party sent to fetch us back. His confidence was met with uneasy glances. Still, what other course was open to us? So we trusted to God, and to Ilot, and trudged on, each keeping an apprehensive eye fixed on the bush. My skin prickled, the hairs on the back of my neck lifting. Shivering, I imagined watchful eyes observing us from behind every twisted tree.

I'm determined now that it was nothing, just my predilection for fanciful thoughts.

Take, for example, this occurrence during my voyage on the Castilian. It was the strangest event and yet, at the time, I was convinced of its veracity. We'd been at sea for several days and, feeling feverish, I ventured onto the deck in search of fresh air, and perhaps in the hope of seeing land on the horizon. No one accompanied me: the squalls were brisk and bracing and lashing rain made the deck treacherous. You mustn't scold me, Margaret. I was not at risk, taking care to hook my arm about a stay to secure me to the ship, for the seas were vigorous. The sails flapped and the Castilian groaned, the vessel cresting a swell the size of a small mountain. On the descent of that formidable wave, through the swirling winds, I bore witness to a monster of the sea. I blinked, knowing I was mistaken, that it was a drifting log, or perhaps the mast of some unfortunate wreck, and yet the image persisted, as clear as a daguerreotype. The monster, for I can call it nothing else, was a serpentine beast of 200 feet. Dark-skinned and spotted, its head was the size of a barrel and bore a strange wrinkled crest on its forehead. Translucent, the monster rippled beneath the swell, a noiseless Stygian creature beside the Castilian. I had never been more pleased to stand on the solid timbers of the ship. My heart thundered like hoof beats and my knees shook. I was bewitched, unable to look away despite my desire. Instead, I squinted against the rain to see it. For a harrowing moment, it too considered me, the malevolence in its yellowed eye forcing the breath from my lungs, but then the Castilian shuddered and rose again, and the creature disappeared into the inky depths.

For days afterwards, nothing had been truer: I was persuaded I had witnessed a monster of the sea, such is the extent of my imagination. Every time my thoughts strayed there, the monster became larger, clearer, more omnipresent, my fertile mind ever aggrandising it in the manner of a hapless fisherman describing his elusive catch. Of course, there was nothing there. The beast was conjured from my mind. The storm was the cause, or else the apparition was a manifestation of my high fever. And the same must have been true as we, the survivors of the 57th, marched onwards, because when we set up our camp near a small crick in the darkness several hours later, we numbered seven, sound and whole.

"Margaret!" my sister Evie calls from the back porch. "Mother says you're to come in for supper." While I've been reading, the afternoon sun has seeped away above the hills. I will have to continue my lecture later. I tuck my letter in the journal to mark the page, wrap the book loosely in its original brown paper skin and hurry inside.

It's much later, in my room, candlelight flickering against the walls, that I am able to return to Edward's missive.

Margaret, we awoke to a strange ululating. I jumped to my feet, my musket at the ready, and peered into the trees, but could see no one. Tense moments passed. The threat, had there been one, was gone. All around me, angry gazes were directed at Ilot, our sentry for the small hours. Ilot only shrugged. A little way off, Finnigan gave a shout. Giraldy was back, he said. We jumped rotting logs, trampled low bushes, in our haste to reach them.

It was Giraldy, but he was barely recognisable: supine on the muddy ground, he was tinged blue and enveloped from head to toe in thick slime. Opaque and criss-crossed with white filaments, the glutinous cocoon put me in mind of a frog's spawn with its gelatinous covering, or perhaps a spider's prey, wrapped for consumption at the creature's leisure. Inside, his filmy wrapping, Giraldy jerked. My skin crawled.

He's still alive! Help him! Finnigan urged.

Shaking his head, McKenzie handed me his blade. I dropped to my knee and, grasping at the mouldering jelly, sliced away the mucous obstructing Giraldy's mouth, praying that the man might suck in a breath and be revived. Sadly, his chest did not rise. He did not jerk again.

Here let me, Finnigan said, pushing me aside and taking up the blade.

They pair had been friends, neighbours since their youth, so his grief was palpable.

Scraping away the remaining mucous, Finnigan uncovered Giraldy's face. I staggered backwards, repulsed. Gibbous eyes stared out at us. Globes of terror, in a visage that was burned away, the raw tissue pink and oozing. A glob of slime slithered down his cheek.

Margaret, I shall report the words that passed between us, but you must forgive their coarseness, for our distress was extreme.

His fist clenched, Big Finnigan shook with fury. Bloody brutes, he whispered.

Baxter sneered. Those fucking Hau Hau!

But McKenzie shook his head again. This isn't the work of the Māori, he said.

What do you know? Baxter interjected. You think fornicating with one grants you admission to a native's mind? Ha! You flatter yourself if you think your member reaches that far. It's of no matter; their women cannot be trusted any more than the men. Sly creatures with the devil's mark on their chins, they're little more than beasts! His face was pale, and beneath his arms his tunic was stained with sweat. His chest heaved as if he had just run to the docks and back.

But where is Jones? Donaldson asked.

At that, Creighton turned and vomited in the bushes, although what he had to purge I cannot imagine, there had been little enough time for eating since Lloyd's death. Creighton's reaction brought me back to myself. My hands were burning where I had grasped the slime. I rushed for the crick and plunged them in the water, only emerging when I had rinsed away the gelatinous ooze and the smears of Giraldy's blood.

13 March, 1864.

After burying Giraldy's corpse, we marched less than two miles before stopping to rest, our nerves frayed and our spirits weaker than a tumbler of McClintock's ale. The ululation came again, unholy high-pitched notes that chilled us to the bone. Baxter said it was the bloody Hau Hau, trying to steal us of our courage. McKenzie said it was a bird, a piriwharauroa. A laughing cuckoo.

Baxter had scoffed at that. In truth, I don't know what to believe, except when we clambered to our feet to press on, Donaldson had disappeared. We searched the site and found the drag marks, slithering off into the bush.

Finnigan hitched his musket over his shoulder. We should follow them, he said.

It's too late, Baxter countered.

Finnigan's jaw rippled. He might still be alive. You saw what happened to Giraldy. If it were you, would you wish us to abandon you?

It was a mistake to mention Giraldy. The man's fate was too fresh, the image of that glutinous coffin too gruesome, and the men all found something of interest on the ground.

For Christ's sake! Finnigan cursed.

We can't keep doing this, Ilot whined.

What do you propose? Finnigan demanded.

Make camp, set sentries, and wait for the garrison to find us.

Ilot's right, Baxter said. While we're on the move, we're vulnerable.

What if the garrison isn't looking for us? Finnigan asked, his voice soft for a big man. What if they already reckon us dead?

No one answered him, and the eerie ululation commenced again.

20 March, 1864.

I am ashamed to say that this morning two of our number left us, Margaret, one drifting away into the bush, and the other taking his own life. Perhaps Donaldson is responsible, his body turning up at the edge of the camp yesterday, wrapped in its corrosive slime cocoon. Finnigan postulated that the shock of our compatriot's discovery overwhelmed them, although what other outcome did they expect once we spied the poor man's boot marks in the mud? I do not want to imagine what passed through Donaldson's mind as he was dragged from us through the undergrowth. What must it be like to be drowned in mucous?

Why didn't he scream? Ilot asked.

It is a question we have all been asking.

He had been gone six days, so Finnigan and I buried him yesterday without preamble. I concede the task was herculean. More than once I had to put up my trowel. These days, I am a new-born foal, my arms have gotten so spindly. Even standing is an effort: my legs wobble like an infant. We are starving. Knowing something of the Māori ways, McKenzie has foraged the nearby forest, but the sodden roots and berries he's found could scarce sustain a rabbit, let alone a group of famished men. I ate the fat white caterpillar he offered me, greasy saliva welling in my mouth as I swallowed. It was putrid.

Ah, Margaret, what I would not give for one of your scones now? My mouth waters at the thought.

It took the five of us the better part of today to bury the man who took his own life. I do not write his name here out of respect for what we of the 57th regiment have been through together, nevertheless, it is hard not to think of him as the lowest of men. Your father would surely deem him a miserable sinner.

Although, I hope Grey and his soldiers find us soon, because each night, when darkness falls with its shifting mist, and the unspeakable ululation begins again in earnest, I rather envy the sinner his slumber.

There is no need for alarm, dearest Margaret. I do not mean to kill myself. I only wish I could be gone from here, transported in an instant, back to England and to you, for New Zealand is the wildest, most desolate of places.

Do you recall my first impressions as I sat on the deck of the Cordelia and admired the perfect cone of the mountain at New Plymouth? I felt certain the peak was intended as a beacon to the gods. You will forgive me if I laugh aloud, for I fear only Lucifer took up the call. We are surely in hell. For days we have been assaulted by a relentless, unpitying deluge. It is as if the mountain has captured the clouds, holding them against its flanks with the express purpose of torturing us. The forest that surrounds us is thick and dense and water drips everywhere. Sometimes I wonder, was I ever dry? Then, there are the swarms of vicious black flies that consume the miserable flesh that remains to us. When the flies have supped their fill, fat welts rise at the site. We scratch at the bites with our fingernails, desperate to purge the murderous itching. It is enough to drive a man insane. Of all of us, McKenzie suffers the least, rubbing the leaves of a plant he calls ngāio on his skin. He claims it is an old wives' tale; a Māori remedy against the flies.

The rest of us prefer to endure.

I look up. Dark shadows hover in the corners of my room. The house is quiet, the household long since gone to their beds. With bleary eyes and shaking hands, I turn the pages. Only a handful of entries remain. Dare I read on? No, I should wait until the morn, where the golden sunlight and smell of baking bread will dampen my fears.

Sliding the journal onto my nightstand, I pull my nightdress over my head and slip beneath my covers, reassuring myself that all will be well. Why else would I have received the journal? Edward will have sent it ahead to prepare me. Surely, he is safe in the garrison, yet weakened still from his ordeal. I must not fret because as soon as he is sufficiently recovered, Governor Grey will transport him back to England, *back to me.*

Morning is too far away. My candle is good for another hour, so I lift the journal onto my knees and read on.

28 March, 1864.

Ilot has gone and more drag marks have appeared only yards from where I slept. And always that damnable ululating. Incessant. On and on. Driving us to distraction. Finnigan and McKenzie are urging us to leave. Baxter refuses. We are too weak to withstand an assault, anyway.

Baxter said if the Hau Hau were to bring Ilot back on the morn, he might be tempted to eat him. A poor joke, but still we laughed.

It isn't the Hau Hau, McKenzie insisted.

We shook our heads. What does he know?

Last night, when I slept, I dreamed of home, of the lane where I plucked a honeysuckle flower from the hedgerow and tucked it in your hair. Do you think of me still, Margaret? Will anyone read these words? Is it cowardly of me to admit I am too tired and too heartsick to hope?

30 March, 1864.

Somehow McKenzie's Māori woman has found us. She came creeping into the camp at twilight. Finnigan, jumpy as all hell, almost blew her head off with his musket. It was lucky he didn't because, wondrous of wondrous events, she brought with her a basket of sweet potatoes. I bit right into one, the rough purple skin included, eating the hard flesh as if it were an apple. My stomach has shrunk so much, I could only eat one, but I swear I had never eaten anything so delicious.

Ask her when Grey's men will get here, Baxter demanded, his mouth full of the tuber.

McKenzie spoke to her in the skipping sing-song tones of her native language. The woman shook her head and pulled on McKenzie's arm, urging him to come away.

She says we have to leave, McKenzie said. We need to go now, tonight. She says unspeakable things dwell here. Evil kehua-spirits.

Baxter's eyes narrowed in suspicion. Why is she here then? Are the Hau Hau so impatient to wrap us in their slime-filled cocoons that they've sent her to lure us to our deaths?

No, McKenzie said. She says the Hau Hau went east to the coast, taking the head of our chief with them. She says Governor Grey took the soldiers from the garrison and followed them.

Baxter cackled. For someone not aligned with the Hau Hau, she knows a lot, he said.

The ululating started up, strident and melancholy. The woman's eyes grew wide. She tugged at McKenzie's hand, speaking quickly in his ear.

Bad omen. I'm going with her, McKenzie said abruptly. You can stay if you want.

I'll come, said Finnigan. He grasped at a tree trunk, using it to support his weight as he clambered to his feet.

She's with those butchers, I'm telling you, Baxter hissed. She'll get you both killed.

Finnigan and McKenzie looked at me. Chatfield?

I wanted to go with them, but without Baxter? We were the 57th. Eleven years we'd been together, from Inkerman and Sevastapol to Malta and India, and finally across the world to New Zealand. Die Hards, they called us. Someone had to stay with him. Since Finnigan and McKenzie had declared they would go, there was no one else.

Finnigan saw me hesitate. I'll send a party back for you both, he said. I'll do it the moment we arrive at the garrison. You have my word.

They departed before I had wished them Godspeed, the three of them turning and slipping into the bracken. All that remained of them were three small potatoes.

Fools. The Hau Hau will have them. They'll be dead before daybreak, Baxter said.

I could only shrug. The odds were unfavourable, whatever the course.

In the morning, it was Baxter who was gone, the skids of his boots trailing off into the bush.

My candle flickers. Tears stream down my face.

Please, no.

I put the journal aside and wrap my arms around my body, determined not to read another word. But in the end I do, if only to accompany him in spirit, because I cannot bear to think of Edward all alone.

April, 1864

It has been four days, or is it five, since Finnigan and McKenzie left for the garrison. I have counted the hours, trying to determine when they might arrive. How long would it take them to find their way back? Three days? Four? How long to send a search party? Should I expect them soon? Baxter has been back since yesterday, wrapped in his glutinous casing. I can see his eyes bulging through the slime as he lies beside me. Sometimes, I see them follow me. I'd bury him, but I can barely stand. He's a quiet companion with his mouth full of mucous.

One moment, I fear no one will come for me, and then, in the next, I fear they will.

I'm afraid to fall asleep.

Well, I cannot complain for the lack of adventure. How many men can claim to have seen a sea monster? Although, if I had wanted rain I might have stopped at home.

Speak to me of home, Margaret. I would hear about your day. Is the honeysuckle still in flower? What of your father? How was his sermon last Sunday? Did anyone snore? Of course, I am teasing. I'm sure it was very fine. I'm so very sorry I missed it. Perhaps I will be home for Christmas. That is a blessed thought. But the light will be gone soon, so I will stop my writing now.

My fingers quake and I turn the page. Edward's last entry. The words leap from the paper, and I gasp, clapping my hands to my mouth. The journal clatters to the floor. It doesn't matter that I cannot see his hand, because I cannot unsee the words.

Margaret, the ululation. They're coming.

BIOGRAPHIES
(IN ORDER OF APPEARANCE)

STEVE PROPOSCH, CHRISTOPHER SEQUEIRA & BRYCE STEVENS are the co-editors and creators of the award-winning Cthulhu Deep Down Under (CDDU) concept. Their decision to collaborate on a rolling series of anthologies under the group moniker 'Horror Australis' reflects their belief that the most exciting opportunities for southern equatorial genre fiction lie ahead. The team both individually and in collaboration has contributed to Terror Australis: The Australian Horror and Fantasy Magazine, Bloodsongs magazine, The Australian Horror Writers Association, a series of short-run horror comics under the Sequence Publications banner, and more. CDDU volumes one and two are available now, and volume three is set for release in 2019.

STEVE SANTIAGO became a fan of all things weird at an early age and that attraction has never stopped. He graduated with a BA in Graphic Design and has over 20 years of experience working as a full-time graphic designer in California. The past few years he has been able to devote most of his time to illustrating and photoshopping covers and interior art for anthologies, magazines, ezines, CD covers, board game art and concept art for a Lovecraftian film. As a freelancer, Steve has created art/designs for clients from as far away as Australia, Germany, Hungary, U.K., and the Netherlands—illustrator-steve.com

J.C. HART is a lover of pizza, coffee, and zombies (in no particular order). She was raised on a healthy diet of horror, science fiction, and fantasy, and despite many attempts by various English teachers has refused to budge on her position that these are the best genres ever. When she's not raising her horde of wonderfully creepy children or dreaming of the day she'll have an army of ninja kittens, she's writing speculative fiction, or binging on TV, movies, and games. She also happens to be a Sir Julius Vogel Award winner and was a finalist in the 2014 Australian Shadows Awards. You can find her on twitter @JCHart, instagram at just.cassie.hart, or at her website just-cassie.com

LUCY SUSSEX was born in Christchurch, New Zealand. She has abiding interests in women's lives, Australiana, and crime fiction. Her award-winning fiction includes the novel, *The Scarlet Rider* (1996, reprint Ticonderoga 2015). She has five short story collections. Her *Women Writers and Detectives in the Nineteenth Century* (2012) examines the mothers of the mystery genre. *Blockbuster: Fergus Hume and The Mystery of a Hansom Cab* (Text), won the 2015 Victorian Community History Award and was shortlisted for the Ngaio Marsh Award. She is currently a Creative Fellow at the State Library of Victoria.

DAN RABARTS is an award-winning short fiction author and editor, recipient of New Zealand's Sir Julius Vogel Award for Best New Talent in 2014. His science fiction, dark fantasy and horror short stories have been published in numerous venues around the world, including *Beneath Ceaseless Skies, StarShipSofa* and *The Mammoth Book of Dieselpunk*. Together with Lee Murray, he co-edited the anthologies *Baby Teeth - Bite-sized Tales of Terror*, winner of the 2014 SJV for Best Collected Work and the 2014 Australasian Shadows Award for Best Edited Work, and *At The Edge*, a collection of Antipodean dark fiction, which won the SJV for Best Edited Work in 2017. His novella *Tipuna Tapu* won the Paul Haines Award for Long Fiction as part of the Australasian Shadows Awards in 2017. *Hounds of the Underworld*, Book 1 of the crime/horror series *The Path of Ra*, co-written with Lee Murray and published by Raw Dog Screaming Press (2017), is his first novel. Book 2, *Teeth of the Wolf*, is due out soon. Find out more at dan.rabarts.com

JANE PERCIVAL lives with her husband, Ben, at rural South Head, adjacent to the Kaipara Harbour. The notion of the unpredictability of the natural world is a thread that runs through many of her short stories, and in keeping with many New Zealand writers, her narratives often touch on a person's feelings of loneliness and isolation, and explore the ways that people interact with their surroundings, which in turn, can shape their thoughts and actions. Jane's first introduction to speculative fiction was an Edgar Allan Poe anthology discovered on her parents' book shelf when she was young, and as a teenager and young adult, she devoured with relish, any fantasy, horror, or science fiction story she could lay her hands on. The creepiness of H. P. Lovecraft's classic horror stories has always rested heavily on her mind. The suggestion that there is only a thin veil between our safe and settled lives and the other…a world of terror and chaos…this is enough to arouse fear in anyone. Jane has an occasional blog, which can be found at https://heni-irihapeti.com/

DEBBIE AND MATT COWENS are Kapiti-based writers and teachers. They wrote the award-winning horror anthology of adapted Katherine Mansfield short stories, *Mansfield with Monsters*. Matt is also a podcast fiction voice artist, chilli-grower, and he designed and illustrated the card games *Dig*, *Mob* and *Cow*. Debbie's short story *Caterpillars* won the AHWA Shadow award for Best Short Story in 2014 and her novel *Murder and Matchmaking* is a mashup of Jane Austen and Sherlock Holmes.

GRANT STONE's stories have appeared in *Island, Strange Horizons, Andromeda Spaceways* inflight magazine, and have twice won the Sir Julius Vogel Award.

DAVID KURARIA was born on the island of Ranongga in the Solomon Islands. He attended Kingsland Intermediate school in Auckland New Zealand before reuniting with his family in the Solomon's capital, Honiara. *Kōpura Rising* is David's third published story and is one of a trilogy of tales describing a malign, hidden marine-dwelling race named Kōpura. Currently the author is employed in habitat protection by the Honiara Department of Fisheries.

TRACIE MCBRIDE is a New Zealander of European and Māori descent who lives in Melbourne, Australia. Her work has appeared or is forthcoming in over 80 print and electronic publications, including the Stoker Award-nominated anthologies *Horror for Good* and *Horror Library Volume 5*. Her collection *Ghosts Can Bleed* contains much of the work that earned her a Sir Julius Vogel Award. Visitors to her blog are welcome at http://traciemcbridewriter.wordpress.com/

PAUL MANNERING is an award-winning writer of speculative fiction, comedy, horror and military action novels, short stories, radio plays and the occasional government report. He lives in Wellington, New Zealand, with his wife Damaris and their two cats. Paul harbours a deep suspicion of asparagus and firmly believes we should all make an effort to be more courteous to cheese.

MARTY YOUNG is a Bram Stoker nominated and Australian Shadows award winning writer and editor, and sometimes ghost hunter. His debut novel, *809 Jacob Street,* won the Australian Shadows Award for best horror novel in 2013. Marty was the President of the Australian Horror Writers Association from 2005-2010, and one of the creative minds behind the internationally acclaimed *Midnight Echo* magazine, for which he also served as executive editor until mid-2013. His short horror fiction has been nominated for numerous awards, reprinted in a year's best anthology, and repeatedly included in year's best recommended reading lists, while his essays on horror literature have been published in journals and university textbooks in Australia and India. Marty's website is www.martyyoung.com

LEE MURRAY is a nine-time winner of New Zealand's Sir Julius Vogel Award for science fiction, fantasy and horror. Her titles include the bestselling military thriller *Into the Mist* and supernatural crime-noir *Hounds of the Underworld* (co-authored with Dan Rabarts). She is proud to have co-edited eight anthologies, one of which, *Baby Teeth,* won her an Australian Shadows Award in 2014. She lives with her family in the Land of the Long White Cloud.